You Among the Coordinates

You Among the Coordinates

Greg Masters

11/29/19

to Sharon + Dawn

beside a waterfall

love Greg

Crony Books

New York

Published by
Crony Books
437 East 12 Street #26
New York, NY 10009
cronybooks.net

ISBN 978-0-9859267-8-6 (paperback)
ISBN 978-0-9974285-1-3 (ebook)

Cover art and design: Sheila McManus
Author photo: Kate Previte

Some of these stories appeared originally in the following publications. My heartfelt thanks to the editors:

Michael Scholnick, Gary Lenhart: The two poems from "Marilyn" appeared in *Mag City 12* (1981); and the story appeared in *Mag City 13* (1982).

Gary Lenhart: "Mexco" appeared in *Transfer,* Volume 1, Number 1 (fall 1987); and "Two Cats Need Home" appeared in *Transfer*, Volume 2, Number 1 (fall/winter 1988/89).

Sanjay Agnihotri: "What I Should Have Said to Jimmy Fallon" appeared in *Local Knowledge 6* (fall 2018); and "Pia" appeared in *Local Knowledge 7* (spring 2019).

Thank you Sheila McManus for the cover image and design, Louise Hamlin for the linocut illustrating "Mexico" and Kate Previte for the author photo.

To Tony Scialli and Niki Ford

Table of Contents

Introduction

Art is affirmation. The painter applying paint to a canvas, a sculptor wrangling materials into shape, the dancer moving their body on stage, the writer tapping away or scribbling into a notebook at a café – all driven by a human chlorophyll coursing through their veins urging them to express, to communicate, to differentiate their experience.

No one asks. They are compelled. The act of creation is, after all, a howl, an act of defiance, a resisting of the void, a shout to counter the forces eager to shut one up, to maintain ordinariness.

It's nearly 40 years since I wrote the first story in this volume, the days of smoke-filled bars and traveler's checks. It was an attempt to extricate myself from what the Pre-Socratics dub chaos, a swim to the surface. I'm unclear whether these are, in fact, stories in the conventional sense. There's narration moving the action forward, but I've been uninterested in the big moment that transforms the protagonist, the phony dramatic crescendo and resolution. Rather, I'm sticking to an explication that might, instead, simply express how I feel as I pass through – observing, participating and processing as I might.

July 2019

Micaela

We were driving among the final dunes deciding right turn at the fork. Soon we'd be in Montauk. Brief glimpses of the ocean through the low grass and gnarled trees, stout having put up with salt and gales and weird atmospheric pressures that make you light-headed and make love-making out there a little more unusual or something. She was sitting with her foot up on the dashboard that, actually, in the Maverick, was just a plastic shelf where a few papers and other negligible garbage had been stashed so long, too unimportant to have bothered ever throwing out. Maybe we were talking, but I think it was one of those spaces in time where we were silent, not uncomfortably. I was maybe thinking: She's good company. Even if I knew I couldn't extend the conversation to the exploratory realms, past the obvious, into some new territory I wasn't so sure about but that I was willing to find. Back an hour or two I listened to her talk about ghosts and spirits and haunted houses and visitations. It was pleasant to listen while I drove. I told her about the time at four years old I too had seen a ghost.

The a.m. radio was irritating. Practically driving with my right hand on the push buttons, I was constantly changing stations. I knew this was some sign of discontent beyond the selection of music. I felt a slice of something missing. Not so much that I was with the wrong person, though that was always in both our minds it turned out. (When the breakup came, we were able to say the things to each other we had been afraid to utter.) We didn't know what else to do and let those irks and doubts go by, something unsettled like the vegetables left on your plate or the days we didn't see each other.

What it was I was after would elude me long after this trip and continue past the days and months following our breakup. The more I ran it through my mind the less sure I'd become of what it had been I was dissatisfied with. All I was sure of, besides not being sure of anything, was that I wanted more. The hurt I'd cause was like jet fumes left behind in a selfish walk toward that ambiguous idea.

John Lennon was murdered a week after we finally did break up and I didn't have her to call up and talk to about it and say, as now with the stereo on behind me: "Anytime at all, all you have to do is call, and I'll be there" and "I've got a whole lot of things to tell her when I get home."

Quarter note triplets in "Love is All You Need." I never noticed them before. And that song's message – love, love, love – in the light of what had just happened two nights ago, its writer extinguished in such violent violation, was just more pathetic and the album ended. So I put on the Vee-Jay one, the second Beatles album released in America, staring at the covers for a moment, so familiar, even after not being handled for years. The large letters of the song titles on the back with the bold lines separating the sides' selections. I was brought back to my parents' basement, the black vinyl sofa, and repeated listening to these songs, this very copy of the album, taking in every detail there was to be regarded: John and Ringo's wristwatches.

What was making the breakup easier for me was the people I was suddenly allowed to regard as possibility, particularly

Fenya, who I'd spoken to a few hours ago and could call back or she'd call back or we'd meet at the bar after the poetry reading neither of us planned to go to. I knew I wasn't getting in too deep since she was already part of a couple. I wanted to play it safe enough not to disturb their household since I cared too for her partner, had in fact known her much longer. But I knew, mixed up with all that, that this was a chance for tenderness with someone I'd always been attracted to. She admitted – on the night two weeks ago that we'd finally first slept together – she'd always wanted to make love to me. It was so great when she said it. I've always wanted to make love to you. And it still sounded great, I thought, though at the time I was too drunk to actually get past any initial bed maneuvers. Remembering seemed as pleasurable as had the actual event, my palm moving up and down her torso, and just left me wanting more.

After a few days went by I realized I was trying to stay away from her. "I don't want to be in love for a while," I just told a friend. I realized that I'd been having these intimate conversations lately with friends and acquaintances, some of whom I hadn't recently talked to so much, or not of much anyway. The link, I discovered, was that these folks had all recently broken up with lovers. I found myself in this new club and was enjoying the opportunity to try to get the whole thing straight in my mind by trying to explain what I was feeling or what me and Micaela had been to each other. But I kept sensing that I wasn't getting at it and felt somehow that I was violating the privacy we'd shared. All that was over and now was the time, I kept trying to presume, to understand what it was that we'd had and what it was we felt had been missing.

Well, I knew sitting at Henrietta's kitchen table over dirty dishes was part of what I'd been missing, sopping up the last of the ravioli sauce with good Italian bread. I'd shopped the same stores and come home with bread, yogurt and cheese, and as I went past her block thought of inviting her over for dinner. No, I wanted to finish eating and write, but after my stuff was in the refrigerator, the phone was ringing and I knew it was her about to invite me over. Henrietta, with her Nordic ebullience and blond hair as liquid as a waterfall. So, getting the last three beers in the fridge, I walked down the five flights and over. It was by the addition scrawled on her bag, still unemptied on her kitchen table, that I knew she'd just been in the Italian grocery on First Avenue at East 11th Street.

"The difference between us is that you have this remorse and still feel slighted and want maybe to get back together with him but I know me and Micaela are finished," I was saying. "I just think I've been feeling bad about feeling good. Like I'm supposed to feel terrible after breaking up, but I don't. Numb at worst. I guess the loneliness stuff hasn't hit me yet."

And we went on, through two phone calls she received, and I stopped short of suggesting that we, in fact, could sleep together when she continued harboring, I deducted, on a desire for love. I remembered how awkward it'd been when I asked who was to become my first girlfriend whether she'd like to kiss me. A camp overnight, we were on a hill. And blinking back to the present, across the table, I noticed where her nipples were.

I lay in bed with Fenya, looking at the white ceiling. Michelangelo might have chiseled her body out of marble. In what seemed dramatic or at least enhanced movements I moved my eyes around taking in the white room I'd been sleeping in for a few years. Cracks in the plaster, rough cover-ups I tried to fix when I first moved in. When she woke up, I told her I'd been awake for a while, since a phone call that she vaguely remembered hearing ring. It felt good just lying there staring out into space as far as the walls. It was fun remembering scenes and episodes, I explained. It was like a bunch of movie clips in there, my mind. And she told me some dream that had a desperate need for money as its root, it seemed, which in reality was the case for her, I knew.

A few hours earlier she had talked about going out and trying to find a job. But once Camille, her partner, left to go read her poems at the School of Visual Arts, we just got back into bed with our clothes on. I'd gone into my bedroom and waited to see if she would follow. When she poked her head in the doorway, holding the copy of *Monty* she'd been looking through, I kind of signaled her over with my hand, the way Charlie Chaplin does in *The Gold Rush* when the cabin is poised on the edge of a precipice and he's lying on the angled floor beckoning Mack Swain to come rescue him. But my gesture, I knew, didn't have that desperation, just the charm to say, c'mon, it's ok.

We both dropped off for a while. Looking up, once awake and hearing her sleep breath beside me, I thought: I'll be writing this up later. I was imagining I might be at the beginning of a novel and wondered whether I was doing things in my days and nights just so I'd have something to write about. My life and fiction are getting pretty tangled.

Lying in bed with Fenya was nice but I was feeling a little strange about not completing a sufficient period of mourning for my just-ended relationship. Slipping my hand and arm underneath her to embrace her a little, she didn't lift her ass up to make it easier, the way Micaela knew to do. I couldn't slide my finger below her waist until she would order me to stop, the way I would with Micaela. Besides, we had our clothes on. Maybe if we'd been naked we would have begun to seduce each other but I, at least, didn't feel like it and could tell she didn't either. I let it go and figured if she started I'd be able to get into the mood.

"It's a lazy day," she said at some point. We just lay for a long comfortable time until we started saying stuff like, "Do you want to take a bath?" or "Do you want some eggs?" or "I should get going." After one or two tentative attempts to get out of bed, she finally sat up and I rubbed her back under her sweatshirt. At the door I asked her if she was ok, recalling Jean-Pierre Léaud's response to that question in *The Mother and The Whore*: "Don't worry about me. Today I'm fine." I had that written in a notebook. She said, "Yeah, I'm ok, just a little spaced out." I watched her walk down a few flights. I knew I hadn't done a sufficient job of comforting her. I hadn't brought up the fact that she'd just been asked to move out of the apartment she'd been sharing with Camille and therefore needed to find an apartment and job. But I wanted her to leave so I could write which, Camille had told me the night before, was the reason she had found it necessary to ask Fenya to move out.

"I don't believe that," I told her. "That's just an excuse. You could work it out if you wanted to. You don't want to anymore."

When I looked in my wallet, I figured that I spent $15 at the bar last night but couldn't figure out how. There was an empty beer pitcher on my kitchen table that I had walked out of the bar with. It'd been half full of beer when I'd stashed it under my coat and exited the bar. I remembered that when I looked at the corner of Avenue A and East 11th Street, the precious contents had spilled all over my sweater and pants.

I was in bed with Henrietta. Before the decision had been made, after a brief pause in our talking, I was forming the words and nerve to suggest it when she said it, "Well, you want to sleep here?"

"Yes." We moved over to the inner sanctums and she, shy I thought, turned off the light for us to undress. Fond caresses, touching and kisses though I didn't exactly trust the fact that after knowing each other for so long and not ever doing this kind of stuff, that here we were all of a sudden allowed to be doing it. She'd been one of the first people I'd told about the break up.

Uptown, the next day, East 41st Street in the canyon between the straight office buildings and the crowd of straight office workers moving on their lunch hours. Through a bank window I saw a young worker at his desk and at first thought it must be a mannequin he was so manicured and frozen. Actually, being in bed with a woman whose body I was unfamiliar with was almost enough, I mused, to make me want to get back with Micaela. I was forgetting her. She was gone even though I knew I'd see her eventually. We'd talked on the phone a few times and still were friendly, even tender, but a new flood of input was replacing her, or I was trying to allow it to. The passionate groans and affected response I achieved with this new partner in lovemaking was something I'd known I was missing but didn't, until this time came when I heard it and saw it under, over and beside me, know just how much it was possible or to what extent or even to what further possibilities it could go. With all I'd been wishing for, I still preferred, I weighed it out, and still wished for the familiar, thin body I'd known and the person it belonged to who I'd loved.

I missed the affection. I'd thought of finding a picture of a flower and putting it under Henrietta's door with some line I'd think up at the time, but I ran into her at a poetry workshop before I had the chance. I looked in her eyes with a new precious view of bridges spanning bays, but with people around we just talked the same as we would have the day before we'd slept together. Only a little rubbing was any bold clue to this new identity I assumed we'd established. I wanted to kiss her and had felt us both bounce off some invisible glowing wall between us staying ready for tea in the audience jury crossfire.

I got out of there and met friends at The Rock Lounge. There was a benefit going on for the Squat Theater. I'd been making money lately. The whole scene reminded me of Berlin in the 30s when, I assumed, the people there too had this foreboding of impending something or other. It wasn't just that Ronald Reagan had cut off money to the poor, most people weren't aware of that yet. Or that Reagan seemed like any other power broker put in office by those people he'd serve. I felt my sense of abandonment in this loft club stemmed from having a lot to abandon. The music was so loud and so unrelenting you kind of gave up trying to talk. Not many people were dancing.

Most were just swaying facing the stage or wandering around looking very alternative. I figured it was a slow night. I was feeling plain, content standing there with what I'd found to be a comfortable position – one hand holding a plastic cup with Courvoisier and the other a bottle of beer. "The rich man's boilermaker," I leaned over to a friend and said. The cab driver on the way home told me my wife would be angry at me for coming home so late.

"I don't have a wife."

This must have sent the driver scheming but his answer quickly was, "Well, someone's gonna be angry at you for coming home so late."

"There's no one I'm going home to," I said.

This discussion left me on the edge like a cat.

Days passed. I moved Fenya's leg a little off from between my legs. "I'm sorry," she said. I was beginning to realize just how sincere she was always and how she was so gentle and opened herself up to a vulnerability because she wasn't trying to protect herself but responded straight, either with the regular compassion of this exchange or silence when it was something she needed that time to figure out.

"I'm used to lying in bed with Camille with my leg there between her legs and there there's nothing."

Four a.m. home from a bar I was wishing I was with her. Or I was wishing I knew whether the guy Henrietta had been expecting when I'd spoken to her earlier was there now so I could knock.

It was a gray day full of gravity and I sat at my desk and couldn't even see into the window of the tenement facing mine anymore since the couple in there had put up some chintzy lace curtains right after they spotted me lazy morning staring out my window right at them, as it so happened, making out. The Sunday *Times* in the next room would have to wait, probably late tonight before I'd get back to it. I'd picked it up and checked out the Arts and Leisure and Book Review sections before passing out last night, before getting the chance to find out what the weird music playing on the radio was. Almost two Bach cello suites have gone by since I wrote my last sentence.

Well, it was a new season. That's about the best that could be said about the time which contains this all. I stood in the bar and though it was still too soon to have those old, familiar, desperate longing feelings, I knew that this content safe period wouldn't/couldn't last too long and in the morning, laying in bed, realized I was already sick of the bar scene again but knew, too, that that'd be where I'd be headed some nights in the near future. As it was I was fine carrying around a six-pack in a brown paper bag with the last plan of the open Saturday night just ended with Anne and Vito not answering their door, Fenya two blocks ago having decided to return home, not feeling so good, so me and Barry loose on the quiet warehouse streets about midnight with a light snow filtering down. I could have sat on any of those loading platforms around us and opened a beer, it wasn't that cold out, but figured the tempo of the night had us getting somewhere sooner than that. It was decided to return to the bar that a year before we'd gone to together and danced a lot with a French woman who worked on some magazine that we both had planned on going out the next day and trying to find but neither did and now couldn't remember the name of. This night we met a WASPy-looking brunette who'd lived in Sussex in England most of her life, asked us each if we were Jewish, and worked up in midtown in some shipping/receiving outfit. She was pretty sloshed, going around to a lot of people alternately having, assumedly, these same type conversations and periodically when having to return to the bar to get her mug refilled, Watney's, and sometimes two mugs filled, our own conversation would continue in familiar confessional on her part as friendly as travelers meeting on a train through Switzerland.

She swept up once while Barry was gone for a moment and said, "You look like eight girlfriends have just left you." Before, she'd said I had a friendly face.

"Just one," I said.

"Yeah? I just broke up with my boyfriend. He's over there."

"How long were you going out?"

"Ten years."

She seemed so happy and was always smiling and was getting drunker and drunker and had shown us a pill – of which she'd taken two. She asked if we knew what it was, it looked like a down, and then would be gone, once making out with the guy she said she'd just broken up with and next time I saw her would be with some other person. It seemed like she was celebrating something and had mandolins playing for her this night. And a little farther down the bar was someone cute, as opposed to Kim's, I just remembered her name, decadent elegance. With her it was just eye contact the whole night and a few smiles and if a good song had come on while I was over near there I might have asked her to dance.

"All the drugs and the bars and the little red cars/not knowing why but trying to get high" wasn't playing then, it's playing now. Walking past a shop window this afternoon I thought I spotted her inside and backed up the two steps and gazed back in there. But it wasn't her. All the patter whirling through my head passed by like one shop after the other.

For the first time in my life I wasn't feeling crazed with general desire and was apologetic to those friends of mine I found myself discussing it with since I realized that they were. This new day-to-day continuing neutrality, sitting late at night at kitchen tables, was like the sensation I'd heard about of floating up from your sleeping body and being able to look back down at it. At most other times I'd have been anxious, contemplating the method of moving the action to the next room, but now, in this new color phase, I found myself waiting for visitors to allow themselves out my door into the haunted streets to make it home to, in this particular case in mind, Camille. I'd thought of asking her, Fenya, to stay, sustained pauses in our conversation with that doubt. But it was pretty nice just sitting around drinking beers, choosing consecutive albums and talking about nothing in particular beyond "how ya doin" and "what's up" with a few "am I boring you" thrown in and finally "well, I should get going," twice.

At this point I was beginning to slip back into remorse gear or to realize the veil of activity I'd enveloped myself in wasn't working, as I thought it would, to balance out my capsized emotional schedule.

I supposed by not going out to the bar after the reading I was sacrificing experience for writing. Especially since a woman had kind of been imploring me to go, or was at least being friendly about trying to get me to go. During the reading she'd given me what Gary, sitting next to me, had called a nice rub of the shoulders. I was feeling beat guilt and connected this thought to the other instances, like wanting people to leave so I could write about what I should have done with them when they were there. But I let the days go by without calling Henrietta or Fenya. It was easier writing about them. Henrietta had even emphasized, in the last page's kitchen discussion, that she wanted to talk more. Unlike my habit of seething the days away and remaining away from the phone, she was more inclined to call right up if something was bothering her or if she thought something had happened that'd disturbed me. That sounded right. I wondered why I wasn't the same way.

I'd taken to saying lately, once I said it initially and liked the sound of it, that I had entered this new neutral zone since my breakup. In three conversations I had at a new job, I was surprised to find my colleagues seemingly more upset over my break-up than I myself was willing to concede. The tedium of being back at work was making me say things I thought I wouldn't ordinarily have gotten around to saying. The hours seemed like granite steps of a pyramid that set off a constant boiling point release of balance-seeking venting.

I popped open a beer and put on a Steve Reich album and just before writing it thought: What am I doing with my life? I stopped typing, sat there listening to the marimba patterns, and decided to call Micaela and moan about things in general. I was dialing when there was a knocking on the door and I knew it must be Henrietta. I'd thought of visiting her since last night we'd spent a few hours at her kitchen table clearing things up right away about why we'd avoided each other for the past week. It was her. She needed help moving some furniture around. There I was writing it all down diligently in my notebook at her table again while she boiled bean curd, put it in the blender, added miso, tasted it and said: "This'll be good miso soup." She was wiping the counter. I sat comfortably without the radio on, watching her move, resisting the urge to touch her. While she was at the sink doing something, I went over and embraced her from behind and fit myself into there perfectly so that my arms came around her. I hugged her and she rubbed my arms the way I needed to be soothed and I liked the way things were going all of the sudden. Affection seemed to be becoming a subversive act with inauguration looming. I'd been reading the *Times* too much. In the middle of something else passing I couldn't help admitting to her, with another reach for her hand, "I've been feeling so fragile." And we went on to something else. I was a little surprised I said it, that's all. I was where I wanted to be.

Days passed. Reading liner notes – that Beethoven wrote his last three string quartets in little more than a year, transferring some ideas from one to another, and that a grand fugue ending of one was later revised to become an opus of its own – made me get back to my typewriter. Sitting here now, I thought, I have the bravery to continue, which I knew sounded a little inflated, but I'd seen it in books.

Marilyn

On the night after
I can't call you
because of complications
that I thought right past on my way
to your bed and the Arabian night
of not answering the phone calls and
not opening the shades on the morning
whose traffic and double-parked trucks
we slept a wall away from.
We were right there to
catch the alley sunlight
and let it in
part of the progression that was
some bright eclipse.
What a world we won.
Just hours ago I suddenly had my
coat on leaving and on the streets
no one could hurt me.
Did they see my lover's walk?
Are you thinking of me the way I've had
splashing molecules of what we'd done
and what you are
constant as an ocean following me
through rooms making everything
else parenthetical.
I walked back crosstown
like a man before railroads.

I was smooth as lawn.
Half of everyone says, I forget,
but I talked about you.

I woke up when I heard someone shout in the stairway and smelled the stale, tired work clothes I'd fallen asleep in pretty immediately on coming home from an old job that had started up again. I don't want to go into details about it now, but it involves getting up way earlier than I'm used to. Being only two days a week it's fine. My first waking thought is: She hasn't called. But, suddenly the phone rings and it's her. It's so easy to spend the next few days after sleeping with a new lover totally obsessed with them, plotting out every way it can be plotted and stopping yourself from speculating, then going ahead in emotion-spoiled thought routes that lead hopefully back to them. Especially when spring is just officially here and it's a pleasure to be out there in the weather, the sun's angle post vernal equinox making everyone go "oh it's so hot," or something, taking off a layer of clothes to be folded and draped over the forearm. And rather than expend all the energy and desires that the view of shorn-of-winter clothes dictates (here I am back strolling on the about-to-bud surface of Earth), I can focus all my aspirations, I guess you'd call them, on this one new person and not drive myself and everyone around me crazy simply unfocused and lecherous to the horizon.

I just looked up "adore "in the dictionary to see if I could use it to verbalize what it seems I've started to do to this person. It's ok since it eventually gave as definition: "to be extremely fond of," which sounds much better than the first two, which had "WORSHIP," like that in capital letters, and "reverence," which has silly connotations. So I can say adore this person and not necessarily imply that I'm lifting her onto a pedestal the way Charlie Chaplin always does in his movies, which is the only thing that dampens anything about him. I need a person to adore daily.

She arrived in a cab wearing a long plaid skirt (that had a cigarette burn I found later) and white stockings that she said had a pink tone. She was carrying a bunch of lilacs that were wrapped in tin foil and under that a layer of paper towels dampened for the short ride cross town. She smelled fresh. She'd just taken a bath. Upstairs, later, she told me how the cab driver had said, pulling up to me waiting there on the front stoop: "He sure looks glad you're coming over." We went on all night saying those kinds of things to each other. At one point I wanted to go find a copy of a Giorgione painting she reminded me of, but she wouldn't let me out of the bed.

The room was filled with the crying child bass clarinet sound of an Eric Dolphy album she had pulled out and we both just sat there and listened, her with her legs spread comfortably under her skirt and me cross-legged, able to relax with some supper dishes pushed out of the way, piled but not yet ready to be moved. Where we were at first so cautious with each other, talking of our other loves, I saw her loosening up, being less careful over the last few times we'd been together. I had abandoned all sense before that, ready to accept the consequences of this emotional foray.

Without looking up from the poem she was reading, sprawled on the floor while I was in the kitchen cleaning the dishes, she called out something about enjoying being together with me and I made her repeat that because the running water had obscured some of the sentence, though I'd caught enough. I stood in the doorway looking over at her while she repeated it again and I paused a few extra moments waiting for her to look up. Realizing I was probably just being dramatic I went back to the dishes.

It Worked Before

House wine in a reused Bolla bottle with the label
half peeled off reminds me of the fresh warm milk
poured into our empty wine bottles
I'd walk over to get most mornings
from a farm in Ireland,
which story, once I was done telling it,
you told me I'd already told you.
No matter. I ate half your
chicken livers in wine sauce and mushrooms
and gladly gave the guitarist 50 cents
earned minstrel money.
When we walked out of there
the world was a place where some
summers, it seemed, pebbles were easier
to walk on barefoot.
We could have been etched though
one fool waved our street kiss on
as if we had our fingers on the trigger
of a gun instead of each other,

defying the logic of this city
which squeezes it into quadrants. That's ok.
I remember this as if it were a newsreel that
I've never seen, the way everything that's happening
is as if I entered the wrong movie. I didn't ask for this.
Tonight, you at the end of a jetty with the tide in
and the breakers crashing. I mean across town,
a promise.

We were in bed before dessert. Desperate hurriedness like all good things. She was wearing this full teddy that drove me nuts immediately because it was too big on her and hung limp under her Giorgione breasts that I bent over and started kissing. For some reason I couldn't explain, I found myself constantly aroused by the milky white color of her flesh. I think it might have something to do with my appreciation of Greek statuary. She got up and went over to the refrigerator and scooped out portions of ice cream and brought them back into bed. This impetuousness fascinated me though I was beginning to see a pattern. The other night she'd gotten out of bed at about the same time and gone and made herself a peanut butter sandwich. I couldn't believe it as I lay sprawled nude on my stomach.

But that night had ended with us saying "I love you." I made her repeat it, "What'd you say?," because she was kind of looking into my chest.

Two days later, I woke up without her, which wasn't that unusual but I thought that having said those words we'd be together again that next night. But she was out when I called 15 minutes into Shakespeare's 417th birthday. I left a message on her answering machine. When she called in the late morning having just gotten the message, I didn't feel much like disguising my hurt. I was fully aware of this other boyfriend she had and her right to be doing anything she wanted. I was glad to hear her voice and apologized for sounding cryptic, not wanting to come right out complaining, showing what a possessive creep I was. Rather, I was trying hard to not be greedy, though I did like being passionate and espousing everything to her. The novels of Raymond Radiguet and Henri-Pierre Roche I'd been reading sort of encouraged me that way.

Something drastic had to happen soon and I knew my walk crosstown in the pouring rain was only evening to what would become night. Paused under a construction site in front of the Second Avenue methadone clinic, I watched for a moment the shimmering streams of drops, gray dancing spotlights on the black macadam and the red street light neon blatant glow and the yellow cabs cleansed by the rain suffering in the headlight's progress.

"I've submitted," I reasoned. My days and nights were built around her and I planned my time to the simple formula: If I'm not going to be with her then I do something else. But sometimes I'd look forward all day to calling her in the evening, expecting she'd want to see me, and she wouldn't be home. I might call every hour until I fell asleep and wake up next morning wondering whether it was worse going to sleep without her or waking up without her. I wasn't so sure I enjoyed being in a situation that seemed to indicate to me a part-time passion on her part, but I wasn't so clear if that was true or if

I was being overdemanding and unreasonable. I was willing to let it ride for the time being and see if things would become more stable. I was sorry I felt the way I did only because it seemed to go against the way she wanted things. But I wasn't sure anymore. Once she'd begun, a few days ago, saying those things to convince someone in their arms of their affection, I felt I had the right to demand this increase of attention. At the same time, I knew once I saw or spoke to her, not even necessarily about this, things would all be ok and I'd find myself amidst the magic. I was convinced there was something like magic involved. I'd told her so too and she agreed. So, preliminary to seeing her one night, I walked the crosstown grid, letting the signals of the traffic lights at the corners dictate my general direction, unsure of what I was doing exactly, walking in the pouring rain barely protected by a shoddy umbrella, but the stroll gave me the isolation I wanted since there were few people on the sidewalks to share what I knew to be an actually very beautiful agreement of place and time.

I arrived a little too early. She wasn't home yet so rather than stand in her doorway I went down the block to the Erin Bar for a watery draft and decided to put up with the two drunks on stools next to me punching each other in some perverse expression of affection. With the second phone call she was home and I went over and we had a few drinks and then went out because she hadn't had anything to eat. The nearest place was a jazz bar, The Angry Squire, but two things stopped us from going in and the second of those reasons I kind of just realized. First was the menu in the window, no burgers and everything else too expensive. Crossing Sixth Avenue she was telling me that one of the waitresses there was someone we had both worked with a month or two ago. I told her how I was aware that that person was always wearing tight jump-suits and was sure she had noticed me turning my head every time she came into the room. Marilyn said yes, that upstairs she would overhear her talking about birth control. So, when I showed a stronger interest in going in there now, Marilyn kind of said nah, let's go over to Harvey's, which had been my first suggestion anyway since she knew the bartender in there and was assured buybacks.

Inside that place of polished wood and mirrors and waiters with white shirts and black bow ties, we sat comfortably, left alone at the end of the bar with the waiters standing nearby, huddled, waiting for their drinks or just hanging around together on slow nights like this one. Things were going as fine as we'd both come to expect, chatting away, me helping her finish her fries after telling her I wasn't hungry. Each of us were into our second drinks when the jerk with the cowboy hat standing on the other side of Marilyn began talking to her.

That was ok for a while. I was disturbed at the interruption in our privacy, which I cherished, but I wasn't about to get carried away with indignancy. But as their chat went on I began to get a little impatient and, truth be told, when Marilyn got around to introducing me, I only feebly extended my left hand to meet the minimum of sociability, obviously telling the guy I wasn't interested and if he had any compassion he'd leave. Marilyn and the lunk continued in their soft-voiced neighborhood talk leaving me stranded and feeling neglected. I knew I could join in their conversation at any time, though the creep wasn't saying anything to include me and Marilyn wasn't touching me reassuredly or even saying anything to me either. I had to wonder whether she was testing me or if I was being foolish and could just be quiet for a while. Here was anger brewing inside me and I got up suddenly off my barstool to take a little walk and found the bathroom, though I didn't need to do anything in there. I stood inside a moment hoping no one else would come in so I wouldn't have to pretend anything and tried to calm down. There was nothing to be done. Returning to the bar I assumed my same humiliating role on the barstool. Nothing changed. When the bartender came over and poured some more Stolichnaya into my glass I waved him off so the pour didn't reach the top and I thought that was sad and indicated something.

When I couldn't take it anymore, not knowing what else to do, and not wanting to do anything but, I got up, put my coat on, said "I'm sorry, I'll see you later" to Marilyn, who had turned her head in the mild commotion, and I stormed out of there like it was a Russian winter. I kept up that pace the whole long walk home, knowing I'd drunk a little too much to think it through clearly, fascinated with these new emotions of suddenness and anger that were railroading around up there in my mind and unsure, as usual, the whole time as to whether I was doing the right thing.

But that was the point. It'd been weeks since I stopped caring about what was right or not. So, mixed in there were regret at possibly having just screwed everything up, but I knew as well there had to be some sort of confrontation and I was willing to instigate it.

As soon as I was home I took my clothes off and climbed into bed, glad to be there. The phone rang and I had already decided to accept the blame.

"I've been home two minutes. What took you so long?"

I explained and she listened and she apologized for her part and I did for mine. Back on the street I wasn't that surprised to find so many cabs cruising at 2 a.m. I took one of them back to her, waiting on her front stairs with a glass of beer and a half-smoked cigarette.

A few days went by and I didn't see or talk to her and I had to wonder what was going on. I felt I was putting too much attention into this relationship, it was overwhelming both of us. Walking back across town after a lunch with her at the shop she had just started working at making puppets and other stage stuff, I was thinking it through for a change. Following the talk I'd had the other night with an old friend I'd run into, I came to the realization that in some way I might be using her so that I didn't have to pay attention to any of the women in the club in which I had had that talk with the old friend. For example, this old friend was commenting on the women, all the usual wanting to take that one home stuff I myself was quite familiar with, hated feeling. And so, reasoned I'm faithful to Marilyn so that I don't have to let loose that barrage of desire thereby contenting myself knowing I'll be with her tonight or next day or eventually, thereby maintaining some balance. How I was so used to and so hated spring without a partner, or any season for that matter.

On the other hand, it was beginning to dawn on me that she didn't feel the same way and that being the object of my singular devotion was kind of swamping her who was more willing to see other people. That sounded fine in theory but this month, at least, it wasn't the attitude that'd work for me. I was like a baby, I argued with myself. When I wasn't getting enough attention I'd get upset. And as much as I tried to be normal about it and be willing to share her attention, it all seemed conspiratorial if she wasn't looking my way. As much as I told myself to crush those possessive tendencies – and knew how important controlling jealousy was in maintaining this involvement – still, my romantic defenses would surface rationalizing the universe into my absorption. I was sick of the whole thing, ready to give up, practically, but I knew most of the blame lay not in her not answering to my needs but in my being outrageous somewhat in what I felt like demanding. It wasn't going to be me to call it off. I was giving myself credit for the possibility of improving myself. If she'd only show a little more enthusiasm. I figured we'd talk about it tonight and she would at least be understanding enough to know I was a little infatuated and, so, off-balance. I'd told her before and even asked for her help, but figured this will help put the upcoming weeks in order. I felt better already.

I woke up from a brief nap and looked over at the clock, 4:30, and realized that even in sleep my thoughts were active and visible as syntax going by like the news in lights on the old Allied Chemical building. I'd been reading, not wanting to sit at my desk to put together the notes I'd taken on the topic of jealousy. What a stupid waste of time. But I'd get caught again halfway through a paragraph and put the book down and just sit there like an aristocrat with an estate before the revolution. I was ready and waiting for the argument and sentences running around freeway-like in my brain to settle away or to arrive at some assessment that could tell me what to do. Mostly, "you're being stupid" was turning up.

What about the sweeter moments? I've been complaining too much. What about the time we were making dinner and a mussel she was testing to see whether was done or not, slipped and dropped right into the dog's bowl of water. And that evening had started with my showing up with watercress instead of the requested parsley. We laughed about that too and with an added pot on a back burner coordinated beautifully with the other stuff cooking she had quickly made great watercress soup from what had been a mistake. And that spill the basil took would have been ok too except its second landing place, after the initial shock had taken its top off, was an ashtray, so that was pretty hilarious too in the klutzy way things were going.

That I hadn't written yet about how when I kissed her or made love to her my mind was completely blank and how that had never happened before and now it was happening all the time. Sometimes, afterwards, I would for a moment be concerned that I could go too far but then remembered one whispered word from her, "easy," had suddenly made me conscious.

In a brief phone conversation, I was getting the impression she was tiring of me. But then something would happen. She'd be enthusiastic again for a moment or as long as an evening and we'd polish off a good deal of wine. That aided in the celebration of our releasing talks. She told me some of the things I'd said to her the night before. I'd been plastered but still felt in control of what I was saying (it was just a little easier to be saying it). Stimulated to a new boldness I let whatever I wanted to come out, feeling safe enough in my love for her that I couldn't have said anything damaging. The strength and beauty of this bond was our attempt to be honest and to keep away the deceptions as much as possible. What stood out from my attempted purge, the first thing she reported, was that I'd said that I wouldn't take care of her much longer. Now *that* was something I couldn't at all remember having said. I was surprised I'd allowed something like that to slip through.

The line had been busy when I got in tonight and kept busy a while, so I figured correctly who it was. This experiment was floundering a little. I needed someone who was willing to devote themselves to me as much as I was willing to focus my energies on them. And all our talk about the need to be allowed to be involved with others was becoming more and more a way of saying I don't want to wake up with you every morning.

I thought I'd had enough. Her not matching my enthusiasm when she got back from a trip to Florida, where'd she'd been flown by her other boyfriend, and which I'd come to accept in what I believed a new maturity, was the beginning of a new set of daily turmoil, all brought on by my own obsessions and ruthless dependence on her actions and whether she called. So I spent an entire Sunday – lazy, boring and vulnerable enough anyway – waiting for her summons. When her phone call didn't come until hours after the reasonable point, I had done some summoning of my own, reaching the point of strength necessary to begin the mental preparations for pulling out. By the time I got over to see her a day later, my determination was interfered with by her call that had her asking me to come over. At that point I had the anger to refuse. But my will had been weakened and the week's plans were being filled in.

Lying on the bed, she asked, "What?" as I looked up and over to nothing.

"Well, I was wondering whether to let you go on reading magazine articles or to say read magazines when I'm not here."

"But you're always here."

"No, I'm not."

She went back to her reading. I went over and got my notebook and the night continued. What a pleasure it was to be lying next to her in her bed, while she fell in and out of sleep, her body claiming its portion of activity away from the unsure pressures of her day and risk, loneliness and choice she'd been forcing herself through wanting new apartment, little money left, showing up for job interviews that she, and no one else, wants – with my leg blanketed against her soft body and down her legs, writing it down.

Outside, coming through her windows two flights above West 25th Street, the sounds of a few guys talking and the slamming of car doors. Every car going by could be rated by muffler. The Yankees had won a great game: Ron Guidry going his usual six, getting eight strikeouts, no walks, no runs, with pro mass Carlton Fisk unable to aid his team. Christopher Isherwood, in the book I was reading at the same time, finding the apathetic routine of pre-war Berlin too pleasant, has returned to London and met Otto.

The season changed and I wasn't at all sad about it. It'd been a series of indulgent days, sleeping too much, living on money made during a lucrative fall. I might wake up from an inevitable nap and the radio, constantly on, would announce its being 3 o'clock and I'd feel the remorse of the day being practically over without my having done anything productive, except reading. The world wasn't suffering without my participation. I wore my seclusion kind of proudly, though it was partly to elicit sympathy that I bragged about it to my friends.

Marilyn, mostly

The city was outside, so famous, totally illuminated by the morning sun. I didn't have strong feelings about anything anymore. I liked lying in bed or sitting in my one comfortable chair staring off into space. Not that I liked it so much as it seemed to be what I was most able to do.

I had suddenly opened my eyes and couldn't go back to sleep. I lay as still as possible to not disturb Marilyn asleep besides me but she was a little restless herself and turned a few times which allowed me to move also. I had my arm around her and traced a line up and down her back so that she moaned very softly in her weariness which got me to wonder if I should feel her some more so she'd wake up enough for us to start making love. Recalling how wet she'd be and how easily I slid into her was totally preventing me from falling back to sleep. She had to work a double shift later so I kept as quiet and still as possible. She asked if I wanted a Valium when our eyes met and when I said no, turned over comfortably and went back to sleep. I got out of bed as gracefully as I could since it was light enough outside now to read. I didn't see the cat anywhere. There was some flat beer left over in the refrigerator. I'd missed the nocturnal buds of the flowers on the kitchen table being open. A bird started chirping outside, the first sounds of the day.

Sad Irish instrumentals that seemed to tell stories of ships leaving, separating lovers, played softly on the radio. I was thinking about a walk a few nights ago up from Battery Park with my buddy Amory.

"I haven't seen her for a week and I feel better already," Amory began the conversation and I immediately assessed the situation, concluding in a second we were at differing views again. It'd only taken a few hours for Marilyn and I to reconcile after I left her stunned on a corner of Fifth Avenue after work the day before, telling her I'd had enough and didn't want to see her anymore.

"She calls me up and starts crying." We were on our way home from seeing a free film at Castle Clinton in Battery Park, *North By Northwest*.

"That was pretty silly," I'd said walking out, "pretty disgusting," referring to the love stuff, guy gets girl happily ever after. We were walking through the deserted streets of the financial district, passing the monumental civic buildings with their symbolic statuary, naked-torsoed Liberty with a sword in her hand. The talk continued block by block.

"We discussed what we both wanted from the other. I was going to move in with her."

"You were going to move in with her? That's pretty quick." He'd only been seeing her for a month.

"Yeah, but I realized, when it came down to it, that I really didn't like her."

I always trusted Amory's assessments though they were usually quicker than I thought possible. But his firmness was absolute and I admired that someone could be so sure about anything. I argued just because I'd hoped this new relationship of his would last a little longer and stop his whining and bitterness.

"Maybe it's just a mood," I baited him. "You're seeing all the bad things since things aren't going so smoothly and you're making an opening to get out. What about the good things?"

"There's no point in forcing myself to try and make things work. People don't have to compromise when they decide to live together. I was talking to Elaine and she and my brother knew before they got together that they wanted to live together. They didn't have to make compromises to themselves. It's what they both wanted and they knew it."

I was wondering if I would be happier because I was willing to compromise myself. I said, "I'm always bending, trying to work things out with Marilyn."

"Well, you love her." That surprised me. "It's not worth it for me. I don't like Jean enough."

We passed by the World Trade Center and were now passing the old Trinity Church and its graveyard, in the quiet night seeming like a personable spot in the midst of all the office buildings encroaching.

"I'm not," I put in, "getting exactly what I want. I told Marilyn the other day that I didn't want to see her anymore. Four hours later we were back together. She called up and I told her that I would have to start seeing someone else since she is."

"Is that what you want?"

"No. I don't want to see anyone else. And she says she wants me to do what I want but it doesn't make sense to me. I told her we don't agree, but we like being together. She likes being with me and she likes being with her other boyfriend. That makes sense. I just need someone to be there and she's not a lot of the time. I will go running across town if she calls. I'm just always trying to adjust, not be possessive, but it goes against my nature, maybe human nature. We talk about it and I try to defy what we've been brought up to accept, but it goes too deep, I think. Part of me loves submitting to my passion, with this sense of allowing myself to follow instinct. That always seems right. But on the other hand, I have to consider her and the way she wants things."

By this time we'd reached City Hall Park and decided to go to Chinatown for lo mein. We followed the path past Pace University into a corridor that served as access to the Manhattan Bridge. It was like the side of some turnpike with broken bottles and beer cans and pieces of tire and other assorted garbage. A good place to be killed. I was wishing I could film this walk and talk we were having. It reminded me of a scene in Mike Nichols' *Carnal Knowledge*, where Jack Nicholson and Art Garfunkel, friends from college, years later are walking up Park Avenue discussing their subsequent love lives. I'd never walked around this part of town and it was pretty amazing once we walked past a police station, all futuristic like in *Metropolis*. There were people, but they seemed to be robots walking about the concrete Roman stairs that led into the shadows of the towering development. It was sterile, all straight lines, neat, totally designed. It looked like it took some getting used to. I wondered if the people here ever got used to it.

Marilyn knew the bars of Tottenville. I'd noticed them too in our tour of the town and our trips to the A&P for hot dogs and to the laundromat to dry the load of wash Marilyn had brought with her to wash in her mom's washer. There were nine, she informed me, and all looked interesting and to be the only possibility for a night out in this small town. There were a matching number of churches of differing sizes and degrees of gaudiness. There was even a synagogue. "Never seen anyone entering or leaving there," she mentioned. As we drove by, I was content knowing I'd never enter any of them. It was the church on the edge of town that was to be my last impression of Tottenville as we drove out nine hours after entering, whooshing by in the car, leaving the dead under their stones and the church building in the middle of it. Let it sit there spookily scaring generations in its moon cloud silence.

Out for the one spin we'd have alone, waiting for the clothes in the laundromat dryer, we drive to a nearby bar that Marilyn has talked about before, passing two others that I figured we might get to some other time. Parking the car in front, an older woman, anticipating our destiny, comes over from somewhere up the sidewalk a bit.

"That's Ruth, Dave's girlfriend," Marilyn says. This is Dave's bar, an old wooden tavern decorated with ages past fireman's paraphernalia. Dave's fetish, since he was, the tour continues, a pyromaniac when he was little and a volunteer fireman when older. The older woman goes behind the bar as if she used to do it for Prometheus and pours our drafts in grim silence implying that we're destroying the peaceful nothingness of her afternoon. There are no other customers and the lighting is diffused to match the dark wood. Someone looking to escape a bright day would welcome this refuge. We would relax and feel at ease, too, if this somber bartender would go sit somewhere else instead of looking at us from across the wood bar seated on her stool loft, dead silent, disapproval etched in her glare, even in the way she moves her cigarette. I escape to the bathroom and when Ruth sees me looking, calls out the only words she'll say the whole time: "The light's up on the wall by the window."

It's all worth it for the view I have when I come out of there: Marilyn waiting down at the opposite end of the bar, looking my way, her blond hair halo-rayed by the daylight coming in the open doorway behind her. That frames her. Soft baby light surrounds her on her stool like she's just appeared in a flash from another planet. A glass of cold draft in her hand and one waiting for me full next to her. The grouchy barkeep also in the view is just decoration and local color. It's the kind of shot a movie crew spends hours setting up. Where I gladly enter. We finish our beers. Marilyn points out the pictures of Miss Rheingolds as we leave to go pick up the laundry. More glaring, this time from a native waiting for her clothes, challenging our having entered a sacred spot in town with a "who could you possibly be" look, obviously not recognizing Marilyn, for 25 years a native, too, only having left two years ago. I empty the huge dryer with my back to her cold eyes and we're out of there, talking about it as we cross the parking lot and get in the car and drive off.

Things were getting too experimental. I'd chosen to start seeing someone new. I thought it an allowance while Marilyn was away, but it had become more interesting as the relationship progressed. Now that Marilyn was back, I found myself unable to do what I'd supposed would have been inevitable

– picking up where we'd left off. I found myself home at 7 o'clock Saturday night, watching a World Series game, not willing for the moment to make the choice of who to call. Like a clairvoyant I anticipated the phone to ring at any moment and decide my plans for me.

"Hi."

"Hi, where've you been?"

"Um, well Tottenville for the weekend."

"That's what I figured. I called you a few times."

"What are you doing tonight? Want to have dinner?"

"Nah, I want to stay in tonight. I've been out too much."

"Socializing too much?"

"No, I wasn't doing so much of that. I don't know what I've been doing."

"Well, I was going to be in your neighborhood and thought we could have dinner."

"Yeah, well, no."

"Ok, I'll speak to you. I won't call you tonight if you're going to be busy."

"I'll call you late."

"All right, speak to you later."

"All right, bye."

"Bye."

Marilyn saw that she was losing some hold on things since I wasn't paying as much attention to her as she was used to. I was usually home this last week since I too was finding this surplus of involvement needing some retreat. I'd always known that the way I felt about a lover could change almost daily, sometimes hourly, but I'd reached a new plateau of now accepting that I couldn't trust my feelings. I'd said so in a letter that I still wasn't sure would get mailed. I had been able to define it to myself as if it deserved applause. I went free form. I'd learned with Micaela, a former lover, that there were no outlines and now had progressed to where I felt like I was walking around in the middle of a Jackson Pollock painting.

I heard the hesitancy in her voice as she asked on the phone whether I'd been with X these last few days. It was 1:30 in the morning and she'd woken me and asked if I were alone. I felt a little glad recognizing in those questions, and the tone she asked, my remembrance of being in the same position.

"No, I haven't," I was able to say with a blanket of tenderness, relievedly critical of my last week's behavior. Things were a mess but perhaps it was fun trying to get clear.

"Don't you have any feelings?" she said.

"I'm just trying to protect myself," I answered.

I almost let her break it off. It seemed to both of us the sensible thing to do but I lay back on my bed and let silence give me the advantage by making her talk more. It was easier to respond than to take chances with initiative. Breaking up seemed like it'd be ok, but I knew later I'd start thinking about the white brick walls of her apartment and the windowsill next to her bed on which a ceramic jar did nothing but serve as the base for an ashtray I never noticed anything in. It was where I'd put down for the night the book I'd been reading, fitting it between the metal of the window gate, and then rest my eyeglasses on top. Her dumb cat wouldn't be affectionate or come over when called and couldn't be coerced with entreaties or playful hand gestures. The lemonade or grapefruit juice she made from concentrate. Her turntable that played a little slowly. Her kitchen table with its piles of papers and what looked like term papers from years ago and four dusty colored glasses I never asked the use of. Brandy, I imagined. No, I was playing it safe. She was coming over and it could go either way. It was up to me.

"What are you doing in an hour and a half?"

"I'll be here, why?"

"I want to bring you something."

"What?" I was suspicious, didn't want to be manipulated with gifts or guilt.

"A book."

"I don't want to see you today...I'm sorry. I don't mean to sound like that."

"You have to see me. Just for a minute."

"It won't be just a minute. Ok, I'm sorry. I'll be here."

I couldn't remember conversations very well. I thought of setting up my tape recorder for when she came over.

She kept asking me why and I couldn't answer. I just wanted to be out of there. I knew the answers were somehow down in some memory. I didn't even think anymore it had anything to do with who she was or what the two of us together were or were supposed to be. My fault was in imagining the future months, years, and I didn't like the picture. Her tears were unbelievable. I kept telling her I didn't want to hurt her and sometimes was able for a second to reverse the situation and imagine her telling me these things – about wanting to go, not wanting to see each other so much, just wanting out. It was horrible to be told those things when the person telling them is someone you want to be with. We'd spent a week going through this, me only sure of wanting a change and then when confronted with her tenderness and we'd start talking about how Bob Dylan's lyrics mean more to those of us who'd listened to *Bringing it All Back Home* and *Highway 61* than they could mean to this new younger generation merging in at *Saved* and *Shot of Love*.

I'd readjust my rules of order to say it'd be ok to sleep with her again, I'm tired, long walk home, we've talked things through all right. She told me to get my hand off the knob, please, and it didn't take much persuasion and I was pacing around the kitchen like some caged tiger, like some spoiled kid who wants my way. You don't want to be doing this, she'd be saying, and I would be looking at her, maybe thinking, this person is familiar to me, knowing I hadn't looked at her enough to accept her appearance and presence as flowing gently into me the way I could this Eric Clapton Florida guitar solo like an old friend. It was awful. No Cinderella ending, I remember saying standing out like a highlight. It's not you, I kept saying. I wasn't justifying my wanting out with the way she'd been, I wasn't blaming her. I thought things could have been better and maybe if she were different I would have had more of a desire to continue and to work, but I was through, I kept telling myself, anyway, though I'd said the same thing twice to her this week already, convinced I was making the break. We were too alike, responding so immediately to each other's least hint for anything less than passion. There were these attitude barometers inside of us that worked across phone lines. We couldn't hide anything. You really don't care, was the last thing she said, closing the door with a new instant look on her face of I'm not going to allow you to hurt me. I liked its sophistication.

A lot of all this had to do with my having started work at a new job with the probability of going on a night shift – which Marilyn didn't want me to do. I was so broke that I'd asked everyone I could for a dollar here, five here, $50 from Barry. I didn't want to ask anymore. I was walking all over town with no money for the bus or subway. I'd gotten caught a month ago jumping over a turnstile so didn't want to bother trying any more times. I slept until noon the day I was supposed to go to court. I'd go off to this new job and for two days didn't have any money so didn't eat. I was able to tell one person there that I was broke, a woman who'd been friendly and gone out of her way to make me feel comfortable. She brought out some crackers that she said had been lying around since the fourth of July and then reached in the little fridge and pulled out this blackberry preserve from France that some client, she said, had given them. I went right over to the coffee pot where there was a plate and some plastic spoons and spread that stuff on some crackers with the handle of the spoon and munched down a few, not caring what one of the bosses passing by had to think. Not more than five minutes later, after having cleaned up a little, I got the jar out again and repeated the entire procedure. A few little cups of water from the great water cooler and I was content as Louis the 16th or whatever Louie.

The TV went on flickering while Van Morrison sang like bourbon on the spinning record player. I'd come back from a dinner with Barry and thought to invite myself up while he worked in the darkroom. But at the front door, after he asked what I was going to do with the rest of the evening, I decided to come home to rework what I'd written in the afternoon, which I knew I wasn't satisfied with, getting there but leaving off too soon, like a comedy sketch on TV involved with love potions.

It bothered me to compare the miserable way things were going with Marilyn to Barry's progress and happiness with his new girlfriend (he'd kissed the telephone answering machine as she spoke on tape).

I lay in bed and worked on conversations I'd likely never have. I'd stopped being worried about having to wake up for work a few hours ago. I was hesitant to write more about things I'd been thinking, but indulgence was all that was available, all I could afford. Actually, my situation was a mirror of the times I was discovering myself to be a chronicler of. There wasn't much being written from my view. That books and movies so rarely portrayed anyone I would have anything much to do with was finally becoming clear. My friends had been supportive as models these last years and now, I felt, I could offer testament to this marginal group or, at least, exploit the possibilities of their uniqueness. I wanted a bestseller.

Paying rent for six years in New York City had always obliged me to be somewhat responsibile but, for a moment the other day, I'd felt like I could just let it all go. It was too enormous a game to ask anyone to play. I'd been talking for months about fixing my place up and I'd meant it, but now, broke, didn't see it happening in the near future. Further, it seemed most of my friends were looking for work or had jobs they hated. It would be someone else's time for an eviction notice every other month. The city was really getting oppressive. Our disregarded neighborhood, the East Village of Manhattan, which had long been the most affordable in the city, had been discovered by developers as prime real estate and rents had been doubling and tripling. Those of us who'd been here for the last five or so years were protected by leases, though landlords in many cases had tried nervy tactics to evict and/or harass in order to move in this new breed of people all of us had moved here to get away from. Boutiques, new restaurants that we could hardly ever afford to eat in, and other stores with opulent facades that sold stuff none of us was much interested in, had sprung up and seemed to be doing all right for themselves.

"Fine," I was saying, slipping money to the attendant through the slot for my subway tokens. "If that's what you want."

It was one of those break-up talks we were having as I wondered whether I wanted my hours to be edged with these concerns again. After a brief pause my response sounded businesslike, as if we were cementing a deal. We were going to start "just being friends."

A few hours later, Barry was taking photographs of us from across a table in an Italian deli on Ninth Avenue. There were a few tables in the back of this place that was a market in the front with a beautiful wood floor and the shelves filled with colorful imported cartons. Cheeses and salamis were hanging from the ceiling on gray strings. In one shot, Marilyn is biting my ear and my face shows outrage with a smile, glad of the attention. In some others we're kissing or looking into each other's eyes.

I've been lazy about writing anything for almost a year now, ever since a girlfriend I had back in the fall told me right off to not write anything about her. When that ended, I guess I'd just had it for a while and kind of stopped looking and don't remember exactly what I did all that winter. And now it's almost the end of another summer, 1982. To write it down makes it nostalgic. To me it's sad that I haven't written anything about that relationship. That she forbid me. That I listened to her. It was just my laziness finding a perfect excuse. Maybe I needed the break to pull back and become whole again or to feel in control. But it's beginning to look like that stuff never happens unless maybe you pray or sit and meditate every day for 40 years. That's not exactly what I have in mind for a life.

Pia

We'd been dancing for hours. I hadn't particularly wanted to come to this place, a working people's bar, I'd leaned over and mentioned to her at one point, my words mixing in with the loud, unrelenting pulse-driven rush sounds of the band and the smoke and the wood. There was only $10 left in my wallet after we'd had dinner. Beyond this sense of obligation to show her a "good time," I didn't quite know what to do and wasn't that certain how much ambition I had to do it.

Pia and her friend Dynaka had been staying at my neighbor's, all of them Danish. "A friend in Copenhagen," I remember her telling me, "told us about Aneeda, but that she was living with a boyfriend so we probably wouldn't be able to stay there. But when we got to New York..." They ended up there with the boyfriend out of town, on tour with a band he didn't get along with, calling Aneeda drunk at four in the morning, moaning.

This place was all right. A blues bar I'd gone to once in a while – most recently, on my way home from work at two in the morning. For the six weeks I had that job, I'd gone in a few times for a beer, more often peered in the window between the slits for a minute before continuing home. Once, the blond waitress stuck her tongue out at me. The band wasn't good enough that night.

But, being free admission, this was the place. The reggae club a block away, that used to be the Caribbean club, charged $10 and they only wanted tuxes and gowns in there. "Did you see the way that guy looked at us when we went in there?"

I don't think it was much past the first beer that I asked Pia to dance and, the good host, tapped Dynaka's arm to suggest she come with us out to that new zone. I was moving pretty good, or at least enjoyed anticipating beats and feeling the success of moving some part of my body to join it. And there's always at least four beats a measure, though there might have been a waltz around the third set. I had to remember to look up once in a while to see what they were doing. I had this tendency to look down or close my eyes when dancing.

Pia was a good dancer. She wore this content smile and kept her eyes closed, as if she were dancing in some lush bathroom with a vermouth after a good bath. I'd turn to Dynaka to show for a moment that I was interested in her too but she was doing all right. In fact, once when Pia went to sit down, Dynaka and I stayed out there and she opened her lips a little bit, so far from her social work in Denmark. She could have been some seductress in an Italian film from the 1960s, perhaps a Fellini dream in soft-focus waving a silk scarf with a bed behind her and Marcello Mastroianni smiling, getting ready to take his glasses off. But this was just filler to my wanting to get back to Pia. Though I reacted to Dynaka's gear switching with a few second-rate James Brown dance steps, mostly I was hoping Pia might be a little jealous and that she was aware I wasn't paying every second of attention to her. Which I wanted to be doing.

Dynaka wasn't drinking. She hadn't had anything to eat at dinner either and had commented on the smoke the first 10 minutes we were in the bar. I knew what that meant. Bar smoke was something you were either willing to submit to or let stand as an excuse for leaving. It was a ridiculous policy but the bar only served draft beer, and weak stuff too. I might not have noticed but Pia mentioned it at some point. It felt great to be conscious of what I was saying so late. Through the course of the night, Pia and I traded rounds, not so many, each new glass a further acknowledgement of recklessness, some Reginald Marsh painting.

Pia and I stayed out there on the floor between songs waiting for the next one. Didn't matter what it was. Old favorites might make you move better but the band churned them out and was tight and the bass player and drummer worked together as solid as Ron Guidry and Thurmon Munson had, affecting blood in my veins the way the moon draws up the tides. It was incredible. Dance dance dancing. We found more space in the back behind the pool table where a few guys were just sitting around. Some nice-looking guy with short black hair, maybe he'd been in the army, maybe he had Mafia connections, had asked Dynaka to dance about a half-hour ago.

It must have been around the middle of our time there that I began to want to touch Pia, hold her while we danced, even if it was some jitterbug partner kind of dance hold. While we danced apart, shaking around, she looked like she felt good. I noticed one couple who were entwined. Each dance after that was some mild attempt at getting closer to Pia. I'd move in close thinking about just sticking my hand out for her to take but she didn't seem to suggest it. Sitting down once, I'd let my hand, moving from one place to another, brush against her shoulder. I knew all about this from Eric Rohmer movies. I thought: I'm too old to be feeling this. But was secretly glad

as it'd been a long time. At the table once and then once dancing, I'd touched her accidentally and felt it shoot through my
body and down my legs. Really. Just a graze.

Pia was pretty with high cheekbones, a reddish tone to her
face, sleek eyes like a tigress and straight watery hair she
kept doing something with. It was more than just her face or
body. It was more this radiance, her smile, the way she always
seemed interested, curious, always kinetic. You knew she was
there participating. Plus, the way she lounged around late at
night in just a sweater or came out of the bathroom with her
pants not zipped was enough to intercept anyone's meager
attempts at logic.

My neighbor Aneeda and I, in our union, had done some
assessing of her. "She works in the club in Christiana that
isn't so good," was her verdict. Aneeda had worked at and
helped build a place in that area of Copenhagen that was more
a neighborhood place and a safe zone for travelers passing
through. People lived there, she explained. It couldn't afford
to get the bands that Pia's club could. Additionally, Pia's
clothes were fashionable and she'd painted her fingernails in
an elaborate two tone, the nail diagonally split with black and
red painted halves. This wasn't the sort of thing that'd usually
attract me to somebody. But she was next door.

I heard someone say that it was two o'clock after the second
set ended, but this was a night when the clocks were being set
back so I didn't really know what time it was and didn't much
care. There were faces in the crowd I'd kept track of, but it
seemed I was seeing most of the people for the first time each
pause I'd take to look around. The couple who'd been sitting

next to us all night, mostly making out, finally got up and let loose. They took over the dance floor with her flinging her long skirt around like a flamenco queen and he, the ample straight man, taking care of his half of the floor. Fellow revelers moved away to let them own the moment. I was hit by one of the shoes she reached down to toss off. After that, I don't think I saw them again.

I was building up the nerve to touch Pia. I knew it was so simple and ordinary and you could act like you were just dancing. I guess I felt it'd be too bold a thing to do and maybe she wouldn't like it. It was nuts. I'd move in a little closer hoping for some sign to say "yes, it's ok, it'd be great, let's do it, c'mon asshole," but would turn at the last moment and boogaloo a step back. The band started playing an old Supremes song, "I need love, love," and it seemed that that was a better time than most. I could imagine remembering it was during that Supremes song. It went by. Then, of course, when the next song began the moment came when I just reached over and took her hand and put my other behind her and we were out there. It was some odd tempo and it took us a few moments to move together smoothly. Those first few moments, I thought: Oh no, I've blown it. At the same time, I was assessing her back which was firm and smooth and intimated at the lightness of her body. The floor was ours and there was suddenly more room on it than there'd been all night. We took possession like any dancing couple in a beer bar imagining they were Fred Astaire and Ginger Rogers. I didn't even have the time to look up to see what people watching us were thinking. I looked at my dance partner but she wasn't looking back. Her hand was doing something friendly in mine, feeling around, getting a better grip. At the chorus I'd twirl her away and pull her back like a yo-yo and it worked perfectly and, confidently rooted, I'd twirl her around with my hand on her back to save her from the eager centrifugal forces we were testing and extending. She was pressing me closer. I couldn't believe it. Thinking we could hold things off until later (something I'd thought in a situation nine years ago in Wales, so should have known better), I restrained myself from hugging her and moved gently back a little. Occasionally our bodies would align and it felt complete, like prix fixe. That she was allowing it to happen erased everything else from my memory. At the Act 3 equivalent of the song, I dared in our swirling to put my cheek against her temple and kept it there an abandoned moment, which I retrieve, like a miser, now.

At the next table, the two people who'd been waiting tables all night were dividing up their large pile of change. Stacks of quarters were arranged in two columns the whole length of the table and quickly, with the tips of her fingers, the blond waitress slid the smaller change over to the guy, one for you, one for me.

It seemed the three of us were about ready to get going. Dynaka was talking to the guy she'd been dancing with. He was telling her how he'd been in Denmark for one hour switching planes. He seemed ok. I would have let him take us to an after-hours club if he was going to suggest it. I went over to the goofy-looking guy who'd gotten us our few rounds. He was standing at the bar having just been in some argument with the owner. The large bartender wasn't butting in or telling her to hush her screeching a little. He was very pissed. I thought he might have just been fired, which I would have felt bad about since he'd been hustling through the crowd all night with his trays of drinks and back with empties, through all that smoke, too. He went around steaming for a moment, a victim of injustice, shoving chairs back under tables in a mad cooling off. The waitress was soothing him down with an affectionate hand on his arm and after a few minutes, since he was still straightening out chairs and beginning to clean things up, I figured he hadn't actually been fired. When I went over to give him my last quarter, I told him I hoped things were ok. He was still so flustered – his mind in space a whirlwind of alternatives – that he didn't hear me. Heading back to the table I found a crumpled dollar in a pocket and tossed it into the band's tip tureen.

Dynaka shook hands with her new friend and held it there an extra moment with the rest of her body headed for the door. Neither of them suggested anything more than good-bye. The three of us – Dynaka, Pia and me – walked the few blocks home, down deserted East 12th Street, too late even for the drug dealers to be hanging out in front of their bricked-up tenement. There wasn't one tree on my block. I noticed that again. It was still, full of shadows and garbage overfilling the battered trash cans with the flattened rims dangling by pieces of cord.

I suggested a Staten Island Ferry ride but they didn't respond at all to that. I'd been trying for months to get someone to take that ride with me. At our neighboring doors I paused and offered a hurried goodnight to them, both already secure in their shelter as if on the small end of a long conical tunnel. Once inside my apartment and in bed I wondered whether to go back and knock softly. Instead, I lay there trying to remember a two-line phrase I'd thought up in the bar that began:

it's so far past midnight

Ah, I finally remembered, and ended:

and I don't know how much longer I can last.

And now it's night again.

Ana

Ana was from Angola, married to a nice guy named Rodrigo. She got my attention in a bar booth by proclaiming that her marriage was breaking up and that she was through with women. She was coming off the rebound of a few nights with Camille, complaining to me because Camille hadn't returned her calls and had made excuses for not going out with her the last two days. I was attracted to her intensity and intrigued at the way she could talk to me, practically a stranger, as if we'd gone through grammar school together. Maybe that's the way it is in Africa, I thought. I wanted to get around to asking her what the scar on her cheek was from. She kept talking and I'd occasionally look up to see whether Camille was giving me any signals. She seemed her usual chatty self over in another booth or at the bar with a cigarette in one hand and a drink in the other. Apparently, she'd had enough with this one and, for what my next week was worth, I should have trusted her judgment. It was reckless time again.

Too many mornings I'd wake up and have to wonder what had gone on at the bar the night before. Not that it happened so often but there'd been enough times. I proclaimed repeatedly I wouldn't go there anymore. I ended up saying silly things. But my friends there were likely saying things as silly. We'd go there Monday and Wednesday nights after poetry readings at The Poetry Project two blocks away and share the bar with the Ukrainians who were there probably all the other days, too. When we first started going in a few years ago, there'd only be three or four older gents passing time with their shots and half-filled glasses of beer, maybe reminiscing about their days at the university before Stalin removed their professors. Gradually, the younger, second-generation Ukrainians had started coming in so that now the place was always half-packed with these more youthful patrons. Considering how often we were all in there together it seemed a little odd to me that our group never mixed with theirs. I was curious to know something about them. But the nights went on peacefully, sometimes with outrageous drinking. A few of the locals would be playing backgammon in a booth or some of the guys would be crowded around the far end of the bar looking up at the color tv, watching a hockey game or maybe even the 11 o'clock news.

In that place of wood and dim smoke these cartoonish paintings hung on the walls. They made me think of similar ones my grandmother had had on her wall – Scottish Terriers sitting around a bar drinking or around a table playing cards. One would be smoking a pipe and have an ace between two "toes" under the table. In the bar, Lys Mykta, or Wily Fox, the images were of some hero or other, I never asked. The jukebox was good. B3 was a Stones' song, "Through the Lonely Night," that didn't appear on an album for years. I'd usually play it: "I don't know why I love you, but I do." I'd try to listen through the voices and clatter of glasses.

To step back from the conversations, you could head over to the pinball machine where a furious battle would be going on. Sometimes your turn would come up and you'd be gone, absorbed back into the bar-hosted paces, people calling across the room with a wave of their arm to get you over, maybe holding out a bottle of beer. Some hunky Ukrainian guy would be looking over his shoulder with a smile so big his eyes were squinting. People at the bar faced each other with one elbow on the wooden surface, some seated on the tall stools, others standing enmeshed in soul-stirring conversation, maybe gossip, maybe distracted glancing around ready to step away.

Camille didn't seem like she was going to come back to the table. Ana was complaining about the way Americans can be so cruel. Her accent, Portuguese, I'd find out later, transported me to some Delacroix harem zone of satin sheets and sabers.

"Sheet, Greg," she continued, "I thought Camille was my friend, now she ees too busy, she don't want to see me no more. I don't understand, you explain me. In America this is the way people act to each other after they sleep together? I don't know, eet's crazy. You know. Eet's really crazy."

She looked down a minute to light another cigarette and I took the opportunity to sneak an assessing stare, as if my focus covered her with an X-ray being fed into a computer behind the wall that could let me know something of what she was about. What I had liked about her immediately was her little boy toughness. She was short and her dark straight hair was cut close and she was wearing a rugby shirt and her body, as she walked, seemed to contain all this kinetic energy as if she were waiting for the opportunity to slug someone. Her intensity radiated even lighting a cigarette in the dim light of the bar, with the smoke curling up merging with the general stagnant gray cloud atmosphere. Talking about lovers, getting her cigarette lit, she had the same look on her face as a fighter pilot getting briefed about to go up.

She sat across from me continuing on with her complaints, assessments and admonishments, with me merely needing to inject an occasional yeah or uh hum to assure her I was paying attention. In another set of ambiguous months, her attention was something of a relief, letting me maintain a passivity for the time being, content to be the object of her oratory. If it'd only have been a month later, after I'd reached some obvious conclusions, like a new American revolutionary patriot's dream, I'd have been of more use to her, I'm sure. As it turned out, she did get a lot of use from me, but our week together evolved more from her needing a listener and tour guide than from anything resulting from the thoughts I sustained in that bar booth.

I played the gentle recipient of her thoughts like a supreme host, ready with the textbook answers she had no need of hearing. To announce and proclaim her existence motivated her – to lash out at the rejection that had turned up in her stay in New York City. I showed an openness and availability she zeroed in on, a laser of gardened fate. I served for her, in my capacity as Camille's friend, as the connection she needed between Camille and what Poe called "The Pit." It was only after a few days that it began to become clear that it wasn't anything particularly about me that Ana was interested in. Anyone who'd shown the least inclination to indulge her would have sufficed. But there was something about her that I liked that, for the week at least, was able to keep me going back to her each day, suffering her moods. In the beginning it was simply something curious, but as I got to know her more seemed practically neurotic.

When I'd make her smile, her face would light up and her whole body seemed to lose the tenseness that at other times complemented her chain-smoking. Once, in Washington Square Park, she looked at me with that big smile, like an ocean liner leaving port, her eyes examining mine in a quick, happy look that said, "OK, yes, I can ease up a bit with this guy, he's all right." And, for that moment, matching her steps on foreign soil, she forgot all the things that were bothering her that she usually let brand her manner.

As if her smile, though, set off some horrible alarm in her psyche that damned her momentary lapse from sorrow and morose crawling, and as if she'd only been set free fastened to the end of a spring that had now reached its torque, couldn't be stretched any farther and was now being tested, she lost. The spring dragged her right back into different colors and there we were, sitting now on a park bench in the perfect, cool spring evening. Teenagers in gym shorts were making out around us. Guys sat with one hand on their box radios. Other benches were filled with older folks, silvered and sturdy in their neat clothes of decades-gone conventions and board-walks, seated together in a row for their easy chat.

My encouragement, even at its fiercest, seemed to have no effect on Ana. She wasn't listening. Pep talks for her held as much merit as a TV commercial.

While she was in New York City, she and her husband were staying at his grandmother's apartment on Washington Square West. I got off work at 3:30 and walked down Fifth Avenue in the sunny afternoon. I always felt good walking away from my job on 30th Street. Today, with an invitation to come by and meet the grandmother, the arch ahead at the bottom of the avenue seemed in its majesty to have some application to me as I headed toward it. The doorman told me which elevator to use. His mustache was so perfectly trimmed it looked like paper. And the elevator guy, attired in the same uniform, seemed truly happy to be taking me up to the eighth floor. I felt bad about having to make him work. I stepped out into a foyer with a door on either side of a plush velvet chair with a mirror and painting on the wall. "This door, sir," the elevator guy kindly informed me as he shut his gate and door and went back down to Hades or wherever. Ana opened the door and didn't seem in such good spirits.

"Hello Greg. Come in."

So I did. There was grandma in a bathrobe, seated with her feet up on a chair, the book she'd been reading spread in her lap. She was smiling as she looked up, greeting the new arrival, waiting to be introduced.

"Marion, this is Greg."

"Hello Greg. Won't you sit down."

Ana went off to get me a beer. I sat down on an old sofa but could only remain there for as long as it took Ana to come back with my beer. Taking one swig, I got up to look things over in the room, hoping I wasn't being rude. I headed straight for a bookcase. On its top shelf a number of family photos were displayed. A large portrait that dominated was obviously Marion two generations ago, her head tilted slightly in the glamorous style of the period. I looked over at her, firm in her cozy chair. Other shots were of children now grown up and older figures smiling to the camera through the ages from some vacation beach.

"Some of those are from Africa," Marion informed me. "Our family goes way back there."

"Portuguese settlers?" I asked.

"Yes."

I sat back down and put my can of beer on a *Time* magazine lying on the coffee table in front of me. The apartment had the old, slightly neglected mustiness of its tenant. Upholstered arms on the chairs and sofa were frayed past any chance of hiding and there was no attempt made to disguise them either. Marion, lounging comfortably in her robe, feet up on an old battered ottoman, you could tell, couldn't care less about that sort of propriety. Things were clean, neat and in order, if on the ancient side. She was fulfilled to have her memories around her, content to pass her days reading – it was Isak Dinesen today, tomorrow it'd be Agatha Christie and later Chekov and Dostoyevsky. She never left the apartment, never dressed even. She sat in that chair reading or, when the maid had laid out her simple meal, would walk slowly over to the dining room and sit alone at the big table set solely for her while Ana, occasionally her husband Rodrigo, and I would continue talking in the living room. Ana would call out, "Isn't that right, Marion?," to verify a detail of family life we'd just covered. When her dinner was finished, she'd say goodnight and ask the maid to help her into bed. Once there, she'd call out inquiries about the dishwasher that she feared was broken and going on endlessly.

"It is all right," the maid would call back with her Jamaican accent. "Let it alone."

We'd say good-bye and be off into the American night, Ana answering at the door that yes, she had her keys.

A phone call came from a friend in Angola. Mysteriously, the person just said I can't talk but there's been a problem and you shouldn't come back to Luanda until you hear from me. It was a glum scene I entered that day. Both Ana and Rodrigo were clearly worried. But, while Rodrigo was still cordial, explaining what was going on, Ana stormed the apartment like a defeated Napoleon.

"You see, what we think it must be," Rodrigo explained, "is that Ana sold her house on the black market for American dollars. Angolan money is worthless. Everyone does it since the coup. But then they leave the country. Most go to Portugal. So, there's no problem. But we assume now that someone found out about the sale of Ana's house. The Housing Minister's a crook. She's the one who all the houses are sold through. She gets them for the American oil companies who are willing to pay fortunes for them because they need houses for their people and houses are hard to come by. She's bought up hundreds of them. Now with all the arrests going on we figure someone was pressured into reporting all this and they must have records. The police must have gone to Ana's office looking for her."

"How come the person who called couldn't tell you?"

"All the phone lines are tapped. Calls going to the United States anyway."

Ana couldn't contain herself anymore and burst out in a flourish of Portuguese. Rodrigo was rational trying to calm her down.

Second day after the phone call. Ana wants me to call her office in Luanda and speak to her boss. She's crying and I'm trying to ask her what to say, but she's only commanding me to speak slowly. Once the connection goes through, she grabs the phone and starts speaking in French. I'm standing around to help but there's nothing for me to do. I go quietly back to the living room and sit with Marion, oblivious like a statue, absorbed in her book. Rodrigo comes in and I explain who Ana's talking with. He's angry because he told her it's dangerous since the phone lines are tapped. He disappears into the kitchen where the phone is. I'm sitting around hearing Ana's desperate questioning and sobbing. It all seems a little overreaction. Once they're off and come back into the living room Rodrigo explains the new developments.

"The Housing Minister's been arrested, the lady we sold Ana's house to. But I don't think we have anything to worry about, Ana. Hundreds of homes were sold through her illegally. We're small potatoes."

"But Rodrigo, they have lists. We can't go back."

"Well, until we know more of what's going on. I can go back or we can wait in Portugal. It's safer to make calls from there and for them to call us."

"Why's that?" I ask.

"So many calls go back and forth between Angola and Portugal since so many people from Angola have moved to Portugal or have family there."

Outside, the sun was going down, drawing in the colors of the day. Darker mist shades of purple were settling in over the activity in the park and, as I imagined, everywhere else in the city. Ana wasn't at all settling down. In an hour we were at one of the places on Sixth Avenue I'd never considered before for overpriced burgers and some wine. The lights were low, rude waiters who couldn't care less about their patrons' pleasure and tables filled with tourists dressed in sparkling clean clothes.

Ana, in our talking that first night, had stated that she was going to leave Rodrigo eventually, that he was and would always be her friend, but she needed more, someone who... she went on. I never got it clear. I hadn't even wanted to meet Rodrigo and when I did that first evening at Marion's, felt awkward with the intentions I had. But he didn't seem at all to mind that Ana and I planned to go out or that I was seeing a lot of her. I looked for signs in his eyes or in something he'd say, but no, as far as I could tell with my excavating perceptions, it was all perfectly all right with him. At least he seemed used to it and had his own quiet plans to go visit an uncle.

We sat there with the candle lit, Rodrigo and I talking about Angola. Ana was deadly quiet.

"Since the coup a few years ago, there's a lot of tension," he said. "Thousands of people disappeared then and people are getting arrested all the time and that's the last you hear of them. People are afraid to say anything against the government and they get picked up if they do."

When he was in college, Rodrigo explained, two friends active in anti-government organizations were arrested. One was released after a few months, but they never found out what happened to the other.

"The president lives not far from where our house is," Rodrigo said. "When he drives, they speed through, his car is surrounded by police and guards, always. You have to clear off the road or they'll shoot at you."

He explained he'd seen cars get shot at. "A tourist was killed a year ago. Was it a year ago, Ana? One time they were coming by and I was on the road and I was so scared I drove right into a ditch at the side of the road. Luckily I was driving a Jeep, it didn't turn over."

He laughed. Ana was looking down, picking at her salad. I didn't know how to draw her into the conversation.

"Why do you live there?," I asked. "It sounds terrible."

"Oh, it's not so bad now," Rodrigo went on. "It's very beautiful there, you know. The beaches are very pretty and we're a 10-minute drive from them. They're never crowded either."

Near us, a couple had been holding hands on top of their table for 20 minutes with their faces moved in close to each other.

"Ana, what's the matter? You've been so quiet," I poked delicately.

"All you are talking about is Angola when you know I am upset. Sheet. We cannot go back there maybe and you talk. I can't believe it."

Rodrigo looked a little sheepish with a well-what-can-you-do expression, disappointed that the conversation was over and, at the same time, preparing for the expected barrage. The dirty, ketchup-smeared dishes and empty glasses were poised like a ransacked Dutch still-life.

"Anybody want more wine?" I ventured.

There was nothing more to be said. Rodrigo went off home and I convinced Ana to come take a walk with me. It was her last night in the city. Sixth Avenue was too crowded as usual, so I steered us farther west, past the butchers and small shops on Bleecker Street to where I thought the townhouses and tree-lined streets might divert her troubles a bit or let her talk some of it out. Not too many cars were passing through the maze of quiet streets. Flowering bushes clung to the stoops on which a person here and there was seated, relaxing, gazing, taking in the street, not yet ready for late night TV. We walked past them quietly, making our way sort of aimlessly. It was one of those pleasant nights late in the city where you felt like going out and spending some money. But Ana affected geography and all I could do was circle us back around to Washington Square and promise to come by the next afternoon to help her and Rodrigo get into a cab for the airport. I said goodnight. With her head lowered, she walked into her building past the doorman who held the door open for her. I walked home saying to myself: I've got to figure this out. As if there was anything to figure out.

The next afternoon wasn't much different. I watched them pack their bags and helped them into a taxi. Rodrigo stood there poised while Ana shook my hand. With a quick look and turn away, she stepped into the back seat, shut the door and gave me a dismissing final wave. The cab pulled away as she was fussing with her passport and papers. I watched it maneuver around Washington Square Park headed, I supposed, for the Midtown Tunnel.

I'd done all I believed myself capable of doing and whether it was to prove what a sport I could be or whether it was to prove the valor of my gender, my days as confidante were over. I'd brought her, in our days, to Orchard Street where I let her pull me into every shop in her obsessive search for clothes. Another time, every floor of Gimbels, where she'd previously seen something that she liked. Good for the change of scenery, I told myself. And one afternoon in Marion's apartment I sat as polite as a choir boy as she showed me a bunch of snapshots. "Of Angola," she said, though they were mostly taken on a beach with her featured prominently in each in a minuscule bikini. I looked, put them down, then casually picked them up again. Whoever had taken them, and it wasn't Rodrigo since he appeared in two of them, had left the evidence of their obsession in color.

Oh Ana! Oh complications real and imagined that keep us from the simple pleasure we deserve for our desire of it. I thought only in bed could we do our great talking. I held back for that moment, believing that only there could I reach through alleys into the dusty pockets of my worthiness in this dog city, on this corrupt planet, at this our precious juncture in time together. As I sit here now and write it to you, with my wings spread like the screech owl with its meal in talons exposed and dirty vulnerable, I summon up the forgotten secrets, layered under dull days, paycheck routines and other temporary lovers. As the night fills in with lights and the jingling sound of someone's cocktail being mixed or, in the hills, the distant clatter of a loaded train passing on steel rails. I wanted to give you it all. You should have made it pour out from me who'd been so dormant, waiting through all that walking on sidewalks and coffee shop dinners with a final cup of coffee to keep me awake to the threats of the available. You had the key that jazz imitates. And I would have taken all I could from you. Not a bandit but the shared purveyor of your star-lit destiny, to bring you to picnic pauses that'd crescendo with views postcards have never shown. I could have balanced your checkbook. I could have written you up as a goddess of the daily world. But instead it ends like someone taking the needle off the record with a scratch. Angel cotton puff clouds slowly on heaven's schedule through aqua sky bring this message to you.

Mexico

It was time to get out of New York City. The months had been going by as quick as verses in a Chuck Berry song and looking back was as blank as the future. Working for a year and a half had only given me a slightly larger stomach. Finally, with the concerted effort faith gives, I decided I needed another long break from this city and started saving money. A trip was my faith. I saved more in the next six months than I had in the year before that. Somehow Mexico had become my destination. Ten years ago, on a year-long trip to Europe, I'd met so many people, had lots of lovers. The quickness of the pace of traveling – the excitement, everyone always aware of the transience and fleeting moments – inhibitions disappeared and talk always got right to the core. I wanted that again. People in the city had become the opposite extreme – cool and detached, a facade like the city itself was becoming. Neighborhoods were disappearing with new sleek buildings replacing the stores and homes of immigrants and their children, all the spice. The new buildings were giving room to new crowds of ever-incoming seekers of fortune, but what had attracted anyone to the East Village in the first place was slowly disappearing.

Well, I'd go to Mexico and be with people again. Have some romances. I was persuaded to take an intense Spanish course, renewed my passport, got a ticket and a subletter for my apartment. The trip wouldn't come through very far in the romance department: One night invited into the bed of a friend I'd made, but that out of kindness as it was cold and her bed had the only mattress in the chicken farm we'd ended up in on the outskirts of the Lagos de Montebello. A chicken hopped into the bed in the early morning and strutted around on top of us as if assuring us it was her property we were laying enchanted in. I came home a different person.

I can't tell you the name of the little village this all takes place in. It's already on the verge of being discovered and I don't want to speed up the process. I want to be able to go back there with a clear conscience. It's on the Pacific coast and is made up of a bunch of shacks and thatch-roofed huts and a few sturdier small hotels that surround a horseshoe-shaped bay. The land on all sides rises gently up into hills, as if the field at Yankee Stadium were the inlet and the seats sloping up into the bleachers were the rising landscape. There are no markets, no shops, no bank and strangest of all, no post office, so there was no place from which to mail the post card that you couldn't get there anyway. It was the kind of beauty I've only seen before in paintings of views looking out hotel windows at the Mediterranean by Dufy, Matisse and Picasso.

The sun was hot and took a lot of getting used to. It could conquer you. It was seeing crews of men and boys out there every day – mixing cement, lugging cinder blocks around and assembling these small buildings – that eventually revived me. If they could be working out there all day in that hot sun I could do more than lie around reading in the afternoons. Though there wasn't much else to do anyway. Lying on the beach was OK once in a while but I got bored pretty easily out there. What was there to do? I was learning to relax. I could sense it happening in me, impurities slowly burning out.

My hotel had four guest rooms but there weren't any other guests for the few weeks I stayed. It wasn't exactly very formal. The woman who ran the place lived on the ground level in four open rooms with her four kids, two of which she was still nursing. Maybe I remember a man being with her one or two nights. One room just had a hammock in it. I'd always have to keep track of how much I owed as her memory could be a little off and nothing was ever written down. I tried to pay each day but some days would go by when cash was low and I didn't feel like making the trip to the next town to cash some traveler's checks. At those times, there'd be a little discussion figuring out how many days I owed. To pay for a week in advance would have been too confusing for her.

I learned the days of the week from her four-year-old one afternoon sitting out in the little yard with him and one of his brothers. A chicken that had been loose but was now tied up, I figured about to be slaughtered, pecked at the ground as I started to teach the kid to count to 10. I thought at the time that this would be the first of several lessons exchanged but that didn't exactly happen. Once he recited his catechism for me, proudly bringing over his little book and placing it in my lap as he launched into it, his face so charged with the task of remembering, his eyes focused on some spot, so serious like a junior executive, until he was done and remembered I was there. His little brother was doing fine crawling around in the dirt in a diaper, hardly bothering to look over at us. The day was proceeding. The sky was an aqua blue you only really remember from childhood and the sun was shining up there so wild as if our village was preferred, it being understood that the sun cranked it up to the fullest, so pleased by everything at these coordinates, the colors so deserving of the clearest delineation.

We were near the top of one of the hills rising up from the bay. You could get a little huffy walking the dirt path that wound its way from a dirt road, continued up the hill and disappeared around the top. Stones were set at the steepest points as steps and I was always amazed how anyone could manage to make their way in the dark, one probing step at a time, without killing themselves on that path. From where we sat you could see the whole bay. Most of the small fishing boats were already in for the day, bobbing calmly on the still water. Chickens, hens and roosters, dogs, cats, pigs and one burro roamed casually around the village. None of the animals bothered each other and that was unsettling to my textbook sensibilities. Why the cats weren't jumping on the chickens and tearing them to pieces defied everything Saturday morning cartoons had ingrained into me. Things just went on. It was like being in a Rousseau painting. You'd be on a path that led between the few little houses and shacks, round a bend and there'd be some hog with its nose to the ground trying to find the best garbage or any garbage.

Dogs barking would be the only sound once it got dark. It was like drums talking in the jungle the way they'd answer each other from all over in the darkened hills. Like everywhere in Mexico, the dogs would roam together simply part of the flow, not bothering anyone, just sort of meandering by looking for food or some action or to get out of the sun. They seemed to be in a little better shape here than in some of the drier, dustier inland villages and towns. In the early morning, the roosters went wild answering each other all over town, amazed to be awake again. If they didn't wake you up, the great-tailed grackles would. Those guys could really get noisy, especially when they'd gather in a huge, lush green tree. In the early morning and again at dusk, when the sun was lowering and the air was pleasant again, they'd assemble to chatter like a frenzied cocktail hour at the friendliest country club.

It was like that. The biggest activity going on during the day would be one of the fishing boats coming in with its catch of the morning. Anyone who was around the beach would gather around to help pull the boat onto the sand and see what was caught. One afternoon a man in a Rover with Canadian license plates was at the dock bargaining for everyone's shark fin collections. The village was ready for him. The cab drivers took off and returned with full sacks and dumped them on the concrete pier. This was an event. Turns out this man, Pepe, had been driving up and down the coasts for years buying up shark fins to be exported to Hong Kong for shark fin soup. I knew he spoke English since he'd said hi to me. I was almost at the point of asking if I could join him on his rounds. I was pretty sure he'd say yes, but I wasn't ready to leave this place yet. It'd begun working its magic on me and I had to let this opportunity go. I liked the way Pepe took his time and enjoyed joking with the kids and the folks he was dealing with. He offered smokes when all the bargaining was done and then walked the few steps over to a posada. Seated at a wood table, he drank a Pepsi and I had a beer. It was the posada on the beach that played a Rolling Stones tape once in a while. The young guys hung around his Rover until they went off kicking a soccer ball around. It was Benito Juárez Day and the first day of spring.

The days just went by and you'd be in them and the heat would be around you like slipping into tight pants and the hours would go by without your much noticing or bothering to consider. If you did, it was a mistake and eventually you knew that. I couldn't get away from having to think about what I was doing and what I was getting done and how maybe it wasn't enough. But later for that, this place said. The waves whooshed into the bay like blood moving through the veins of your arms. The yellow heat slowed down the gravity in which you walked. The isolation of the village factored into the equation. It was 11 miles from the nearest town, a 50 cent cab ride along a winding road through the final mountains to the shore among the crag, dry shrubs, stunted trees and dirt paths that led to mysterious shacks with a burro standing in the hot sun, lonely, waiting forever. This situation was remote as well from my New York City sensibilities, as exotic as the first moon landing. All these factors were seeping in, not like the sensory assault of walking down a Manhattan street, but in a caring way, everything put there for humans.

I tried writing a letter to describe it, but I was lazy. Though I kept returning to the letter through the course of the day, writing from different places, I was trying to get by on exuberance, filtering all the new sensations into some sense.

There were four posadas on the beach and two small restaurants on the one road that edged along it. I tried them all. The food was the same at all of them, so you made your choice by assessing the subtleties of the experience – the ceviche was cheaper here than at the one with the baby swinging in a hammock among the tables. I was developing a slight crush on the waitress with a limp at the place with the better chicken. But, I was ending up mostly at the first posada by the pier since the ladies running it were so friendly. Then I got brought to Capy's.

Capy's was in another section of the village. It was a 15-minute walk around the bay, but down there you didn't think in terms of inconvenience. You'd walk over a dried-up river bed that, in a different season, I was told, would be rushing with water feeding into the bay, cutting off the section of the village where Capy's was. The hill started to rise. Your legs started to get a little tight walking at this section of the path, but you never had to mention it unless you had nothing else to say.

At the crest of the hill, there'd be Capy's, perched on the precipice. It was another thatched-roofed place, but it was bigger than the posadas on the beach, its roof about 25 feet high at the center, sloping down from there, solid beams cut from nearby trees making up the solid skeleton holding it all up. It was always a marvel to notice it in quick glances. The sides were open except for a railing made of sapling. As you sat comfortably in there at long wooden tables, the view down the hill was of a cove section of the bay, white sand leading to the blue water and rocks rising primordial, like here was the very beginning of the Earth. A bird cage rested on the railing. Inside, a small green bird seemed to be doing all right, chirping away occasionally. The kitchen was along the back wall, separated from us merry diners by a long counter. A big cooler filled with beers and sodas stood near the opening where you walked in off the dirt path.

Capy's was the sort of place that you're always ready to head back to, even though it means, from New York, two planes and a 10-hour bus trip. It was the sort of place that would draw you into its festivities. It wouldn't let you have any side thoughts. When you were in there, forget it. Tables passed their bottles to each other. It's where you got to meet people you'd been seeing around for days, where you'd find out where the yacht anchored out in the middle of the harbor for the last two days was from and where it was headed. The glumness of absinthe drinkers was a million miles away in a different era.

One particular evening in there it was Papa Capy's birthday. We walked in and there was Papa Capy sitting at one of the tables with a few bottles of liquor. With a smile he poured drinks and handed them out as people gathered around him to wish him well. To me he was saying "Good friend, good customer" with our hands grasped as if turned to statues. I thought they'd never come apart. He was wearing a white tee shirt and his mustache outlined the furls of his smile. If he kept it up for another three hours, I thought, he'd tip over and fall asleep. But he'd apparently been going at it all afternoon by the time we came in that evening. Mrs. Capy, busy behind the counter, would come around once in a while to stand next to her husband with a look on her face that said, "Oh, what can you do? I'll have to pay for this with a thousand ave marias, but he's a good person aye aye aye." With her own smile she heads back to the kitchen behind the counter. The easy talking around the long tables lit up the night.

What contributed most to the luxury were the three Capy kids who were there working every night. Alvaro was about 12-years-old and he was sort of the maître d'. He didn't seem to have a specific function, but he'd get beers from the cooler when we asked him and clear away some dishes once in a while. Mostly, he liked to just hang around and joke with the customers, which was fine with us. We exchanged some phrases and between gulps of food we'd teach each other new words in each other's language. And then he'd punch you in the arm goofy like. The youngest daughter, whose name I can't remember and never got correct down there, was a little flirty. She must have been around 11. She did the sort of things she must have seen from old American movies on the TV that was sometimes on in the corner with the same Mexican soap opera on each time I'd look over there. Maybe she got her moves from that – so dramatic, the music always swirling and crashing. Like a little pixie she'd flutter her eyelashes at you then drape her scrawny little arm around your shoulder.

She knew though that she was in competition with her older sister, Alma, who must have been around 15 or 16. Alma looked like the pretty gypsy woman in a Charlie Chaplin movie. She always wore a red paisley kerchief on her head that had little white fluffy balls at the edging which gave the appearance of a garland going across the top of her head. Her long brown hair flowed out from under the kerchief. Sometimes it'd be wound into a braid that she fastened at the very end with a barrette and would drape over her shoulder so it hung down over her chest. She wore cheap plastic jewelry that she probably got

for pennies at the market in the next town. It was her tropical smile that gave sense to the colors around her. The only
time she wouldn't be smiling was when she was too busy with
too many orders of fish to fry. Then she might be conveying
commands to her little sister. Otherwise, if she were standing
still, the cocoa butter color of her skin, as perfectly smooth
as polished alabaster, and her long dark brown hair, all got
flushed in the blooming of that smile.

  This all leads to the night I spent there puking my guts out
for an hour or so over the railing. I'd spent the entire day being
blasted by the hot sun and had not eaten much. And then there
was the mescal. I guess I felt like I was finally in safe enough
surroundings to get drunk. I didn't think I had consumed so
much, but the next day, Jennie, an Australian woman who'd
shown up the day before with her hubby of five weeks, told me
I'd been guzzling from the bottle. She'd kissed my ear. When
stuff like that happens, I feel I'm in a comfortable situation.
She reminded me that I even ate the worm with no hesitation,
something I must have been a little altered to do. And that
we'd taken pictures of each other at the table.

  It goes back to here. There was one little place in the village
expressly for selling mescal. A couple of the other so-called
shops did sell it, but from the back room or they just carried
one local brand. This place that I went in to buy a bottle was
about the size of a bus shelter, just one little square room
made of cinder blocks painted yellow. Inside, the big shelves
were stocked with local mescals each with its own hand-made
label. Some higher-end offerings had more professional

labels. I tried to ask for a suggestion from the two teenage boys minding the shop, but my Spanish wasn't adequate. I ended up choosing a brand that looked less deadly than the most locally produced but not as refined as the most spectacular looking. It probably wouldn't have mattered. Taking my big purchase, wrapped in a newspaper, back up to the little hotel, I induced the gang to try a taste. We each took a little swig out on the balcony, but no one seemed to like it very much. It sort of twisted up your face. Me and one friend, Harry, did take second swigs. We talked about it a bit, but the bottle got

Alma, Mexico, 1985, linocut by Louise Hamlin

ignored and I figured: some other time. I knew you just had to get past that third big swallow. I didn't have to wait long. The next night I brought the bottle to Capy's.

I didn't feel at all drunk but I had my head on the railing and didn't have the strength to move. I was cognizant of everything going on around me and could hear people saying soothing things to me. Mrs. Capy sent over a glass of Alka-Seltzer, but I couldn't even take a sip. A bag of ice cubes that Jenny held to my neck I could only brush away. I couldn't speak, couldn't get it together enough to at least take my eyeglasses off. Jenny and Harris had brought, at my suggestion, their collection of cassette tapes (that they kept in a Champagne bottle carton from their wedding). My favorite Talking Heads' songs were playing, and then new Rolling Stones, exactly what I'd most wanted to be hearing. And I could hear it. I tried to use it to anchor me, to brace myself, but I couldn't even raise my head. I could hear Matthew – a tall, young, blond Californian thinking of starting a tropical bird business – and I wanted to ask him if I could go lay down for a bit in his room under the restaurant, but I couldn't utter a word. I didn't know how I was going to ever get up and get back to my hotel.

Meanwhile, the meal was served. I must have been passed out a while because I don't remember hearing anyone eating or discussing anything about the meal. Finally, as the restaurant was closing, I managed to get up as Dickie, a TV repairman's son from Maryland, helped me amble away. He carried my bag and we had a good talk in the dark. He got me to my room, saw me get into bed and left. I passed out and woke up early the next morning feeling fine.

I did not, however, feel so good about going back to Capy's the next night. I wondered whether to apologize or just assume they wouldn't remember it was me. I walked in a bit sheepishly and said the minimum to Alma, asking if I ordered a dinner last night. I went and sat down with a few people. It was a bit more subdued. Alvaro wasn't coming over and pestering me. A Danish woman I'd talked with in the afternoon was sitting at another table. She'd been telling me about San Cristóbal de las Casas, which I'd been intending to get to eventually. What she said made it sound appealing – bookstores, two cinemas, intelligent people. "That'll help me get out of here in a few days," I thought. There'd been a slew of tattered American paperbacks lying around my hotel and I'd read all the good ones and some of the bad ones. I had a new sense of the novel in the years following the Second World War: They had ethics. Soldiers and gentrified youth on holiday argued with whores in Rome and Paris about morals and attempted in their arguments to straighten things out in the world. There was vast dialog.

My last night in this gentle paradise I stayed awake later than I had been, drinking beers that Dicky bought for me as farewell, and talked hurriedly about jazz, in rushes of familiarity in so foreign a locale, with Thomas from Berlin. As a result, I woke up later than usual, missing the early buses. This was just as well since it meant meeting Gaby. Everyone was getting up or was already awake, which was surprising since I'd been enjoying, these past weeks, that quiet hour of dawn before anyone else was awake. I got a quick snap of Thomas, still sleepy-eyed in bed with Manuella, and was out of there.

Sneaking into Movie Theaters

In Oak Bluffs on Martha's Vineyard, the side door into the Strand. I'd snuck into the one in Edgartown six times before getting caught. It was Elio Petri's *Investigation of a Citizen Above Suspicion*. No one has ever seen this film. It's great. Write me if you've seen it. I took six shots in black and white of the Strand from four different angles. With telephone wires going across (this in the winter, when it's boarded up). The tourists are gone but you've still got the ocean and the scenery. And I tried to capture the solitude and gothic omnipotence of a movie theater not in use but still in town.

Waiting around one summer for a midnight screening of some movie at the revival house in Oak Bluffs, I sneak in that side door of the Strand to catch the last part of *Paper Moon*, which I'd paid to see two days earlier. Slipping in was so easy and dangerous.

The very first summer I'd been on Martha's Vineyard, I snuck into a movie theater in Vineyard Haven run by Peter Simon (Carly's brother) and saw *Citizen Kane* for the first time, passing through some amiable couple's apartment in the process. As I figured it, they shared a bathroom with the theater. They smiled as I, a little confused but determined, passed through. It was all part of the mystery, then.

As a kid in Passaic, N.J., I never snuck into the local venues – Capitol Theatre, Montauk, Central – as my father had done. I don't know that I even thought of it. I guess my mother always gave me the few dollars required.

Then in high school, my buddy Harry's father owned the

Allwood in the next town over, Clifton, so we just asked to speak to the manager to get in there. We were royalty. And that worked at the Rivoli in Rutherford and the Clifton, too. We had to be with Harry, but that was no problem.

Only one time did I try to sneak into the Fillmore East and that was *after* the concert to try to get backstage to see Buddy Rich. I was with my pal Gerry Polci, who would eventually become drummer for the Four Seasons, and that's his voice on lead vocal on "Oh What a Night." As a hired studio hand, he told me decades later, he never received royalties for this major hit. At the Fillmore, we were climbing a fire escape and got two flights up before being asked what we were doing. Now, the Fillmore's been closed for all these years and stands like a giant tombstone. The Jewish dairy restaurant Ratner's next door went down with it but I'd gone in there only once. A date. There's another one down on Delancey Street anyway, a different branch of the family, hanging on.

On the night ferry from England to Holland, they showed a Clint Eastwood cop movie. I had to get myself into first class to buy wine. I had to do the same thing on the ferry from Dún Laoghaire, Ireland, back to Holyhead, Wales. This time for a bottle to drink with Margaret from Australia, whose Morris Mini had carried us through Ireland and was about to do the same in Wales – all the way to her aunt's outside Liverpool.

From there I caught a bus to London, which was a mere $5 for the five-hour voyage. A bargain, so I took it. This was to see the Turner exhibition at the Royal Academy, which turned out to be somewhat of a disappointment, considering I'd crossed England for it.

Two Cats Need Home

I was making a lot of money working the lobster shift in a type shop on Fifth Avenue near Danceteria. Around midnight, on my break, I'd stand on the corner eating a juice pop watching the cars pull up and the party people walk by. That went on for about two months during the summer. I didn't know what else to do and thought at least this way I sleep through the hot days. Not much was going on anyway. I got through knowing I'd quit somewhere in September with enough money sacked away to, if I played it right, last me two or three or however months.

The week I quit, maybe it was even that first free day, all the sudden I became allergic to my cats. A nurse friend said yes, it's possible. Take a couple thousand milligrams of vitamin C every day. That helped a little, but beyond being bewildered, I was afraid I'd have to get rid of the cats.

A few days went by where I was trying to make sure it was the cats. I happened to have to leave for a few days for a trip to California and then to St. Louis to catch the deciding ball games of the hot NL East pennant drive, September 1985. The Mets had to win all three games against the Cardinals or the season would be over. A friend's business partner arranged the tickets and a half-price hotel room, so with me flying in from L.A. and three friends flying down from New York, we met there as excited as a bunch of 12-year-olds. Even Ralph Kiner said later that that series was one of the greatest he'd ever seen. All my allergy symptoms cleared up until I got back to my apartment. The cats would have to go.

I met a woman at the Palladium one night. She sat down beside me and remained so, eventually, inspired by the ease and pleasure of talking to strangers in St. Louis in the fervor of that three-game series, I summoned the courage to begin talking to her, saying something about the ease and pleasure of talking to strangers in St. Louis. It turned out that we'd both come into the club on passes so things clicked and we took off for the dance floor. I think I have an opening line at last.

My new friend turned out to be a biology teacher from Germany so, later, when we were talking over cappuccino and tea at the Yaffa Café (the Daro, with its good Polish vodka, had just recently closed), I asked her if she knew anything about allergic reactions to cats. Her friend, who'd come along, which I hadn't counted on, turned out to be a psychology student and she said it was psychological, I should get rid of the cats and start therapy.

This made perfect sense to me since this problem had all begun after I quit my well-paying job. I appreciated down there in my subconscious the possibility of something going on. I'd just been trying to remember the little things of which my days are made lately: writing a postcard; getting the *Post* to check the box score of the final Mets game, surprised that manager Davey Johnson hadn't rewarded Dwight Gooden for a marvelous season by letting him pinch hit. Later, noticing no one has a tan. I made up a little sign to put up at the Poetry Project where I went for a reading: 2 Cats Need Home.

The biology teacher called a few days later to tell me she was here, after all, with a boyfriend who was a jazz musician. He was up on the roof now playing saxophone. I called my friend

Barry who, it turned out, lived two buildings away from where she was staying, and asked his machine if he'd been hearing a sax player lately. Yes, he called back a few hours later to say. He had.

Simple Drums

I lay in bed with my eyes closed trying to sleep and could feel the sunlight on my eyes remembered from this afternoon's walk. I could smell a faint stink I associated with the locker room of my gym. Maybe it's time to change the sheets. Ok, tomorrow, definitely. I imagined bedbugs, too. Perhaps it wasn't imagining, though I could never find one as I probed what was probably a hair shifting on my body here and there. I was tuned in to the night. The radio was always better this late than at any other time. Something I never thought through warned me about being up this late. It made me feel too much of a renegade, too isolated, too much deprived of possibilities of distracting myself. The demons could relax finally or become more active demanding their penance, unguarded with distraction, vulnerable to the voices I usually feared these moments, this susceptibility to their admonishments.

But the simple drums I heard from my little radio beating from some village on some other side of this Earth at this spectral time, stretched in a deliriously elongated lavishment of calm, alerted me to that enunciation of presence, that beating to announce breath, the most simple beating of pulse to reject being swallowed by passivity or giving up.

I reviewed what I'd eaten today. I don't have much of a memory and not much of an imagination either. That disappeared around seven years old. Too bad. My bad memory kind of flusters my friend Henrietta once in a while. She likes to insist things happened that I can't remember at all, but it's not particularly upsetting to me. I'll say, did you see *Charge of the Light Brigade.* And she'll say, yes, with you.

I have to do better. I'd almost given in to the urge to go out at 11 to buy ice cream. "Doesn't that keep you up?" Barry said from the airport as we chatted before his flight to Amsterdam. "I have to get off and go buy that magazine."

We'd talked about an article on a designer being compared to Alexey Brodovich but neither of us were much impressed by him. Years ago, we would have talked until the final boarding call. Well, that's how things change. I'd just about given up wanting to make sense of anything. That was just my need to control, to be in charge. And I was trying to relinquish that urgency. That stranglehold on my conscience and every particle exploding by the micro-second inside my mitochondria.

"Go buy the magazine," I said. "It sucks but you might enjoy the reporting of the photography shoot. You know some of the models. And I think the building they describe is the one you used to work in with Tracy."

Barry was a photographer. We'd just been talking last night about how poor we were. I'd proposed that we didn't go after the big things because we didn't believe enough in ourselves. Myself, I corrected myself. Some psychological barrier kept us from believing we were qualified to attain more than the subsistence we'd been etching out for years. I was sort of a writer.

"We haven't played the game," I said. "We've never schmoozed the way you're supposed to. Been aggressive. We're both just so turned off to that. I've always told myself it's not for me. And I took pride in not submitting or whatever it is. But now I question that stance. I think it's a way of remaining detached and unresponsive."

"I don't know," Barry said.

I don't remember what he said but he sort of agreed with enough of a waver to not be totally agreeable. What would be the sense of that. We did enough cheerleading for each other that we could afford to stand our separate grounds once in a while. More often now than in the past. I thought it was a healthy thing. I'd spent too much time being agreeable. We'd had painful arguments on two different trips to Belgium. I thought it would become a pattern. But it was just my awkward way of fighting for my life. Inappropriate was sort of a flag for me. I'd been waving it since my first bell bottoms.

In Belgium I was getting past gestures into enunciation. Barry was driving, Marjolein riding shotgun with me in the backseat making some crude remark that revealed the resentment I'd carried over from the states. It had to do with being deprived and wanting everyone to fill the emptiness I felt inside. But I wouldn't get to that until another few months of therapy.

I was trying to leave a romantic phase. I'd just begun to understand how deluded I'd kept myself by living in fantasies. And, for whatever reason, I was tired of exultation. I didn't have the energy for it anymore. Or the drive. As a matter of fact, I think I'm trying to flat out reject it. Except for wonder. I don't want to create a fiction. I'm at the beginning of a story of which I don't know the outcome. I'm driven by the fact that I have to write what no one's described yet. My hope is that what I have to say might help someone connect for a while. Though my real reason is I like attention. And something worthwhile should come out of being so broke.

My whole life has been a scramble to find in books, art, movies and poetry something that speaks of my experience, resembles something of what I'm going through. I needed to link up, to identify, to find heroes who could make something out of what I couldn't. I was looking for fellow sufferers and found some. But these words and expressions would only salve for a time. It's finally dawned on me that it's me that has to do it. It's my responsibility.

And this is my note to throw out all the vegetables that have been rotting in the refrigerator. Tomorrow. As I wash the sheets.

The Visitor

Occasionally, I get a call from someone who has read my stories and believes that by seeing me they might solve some of the questions and problems that have been bothering them. If I need a break from the manuscripts and piles of paper that surround me, I agree to see them. The truth is I need the encounters. The reality they bring me is oftentimes refreshing after hours of being absorbed in the re-creations of my writing. Everyone has something to say. Because I write so much about the intimacies of people who for some reason talk freely to me, my readers take this as a sign that I can help them. Or at least they feel that I'm a good listener. As if something might be gained or their souls soothed by pouring out their heart to me. It is, of course, often the case that some good comes of these encounters – for that person and for me as well. Though I am now an old man I am not past learning.

A young man, I'll call him David, wrote me a pleasant letter and I responded with an invitation to call me. We arranged a meeting at my apartment and he arrived promptly. When I opened the door to receive him, I was startled by the bouquet he held in his hand and extended out to me by way of greeting. Escorting him in, I had him sit and make himself comfortable while I went into the kitchen to find a vase. He was a healthy-looking young man of about 40 years. His hair was long in the back but not unkempt. His wire-rimmed eyeglasses were of the type I remember first seeing on young men talking wildly over coffee in the cafes of Warsaw. On reentering I saw his eyes surveying the room like a child's in a candy store.

"Well, my friend, here it is. These stacks of paper keep me busy. This pile is a stack of stories I'm busy translating from Yiddish into English. These are translations into other languages. Here I have filed copies of the *Jewish Daily Forward* in which my stories appear. It's quite a collection. In this stack, God help me, are letters I have yet to answer. Someday I'll get through it. Or I'll have to write them from the beyond. Here, this is business matters: contracts, rights, royalties, invitations to give readings, speaking tours. I'm flattered, of course, but how could one man show up everywhere these people expect me to. And then I'm supposed to be writing stories at the same time. But, forgive me, can I get you anything to drink?"

"No, thank you. I'm fine. Thank you for seeing me."

"Oh, well," I stammered, "I like to keep in touch with the younger writers. Did you bring any of your stories?"

"Yes. I'll leave this with you. Perhaps you'll enjoy them. I hope you will. If you get around to reading them. I see how busy you are."

"It will be a pleasure to look at them," I assured him, wondering if, in fact, I would ever get to his writing.

"Mr. Singer," he continued, not wasting any time, "I've read most of your books. The writing seems at first to be so simple. But you penetrate to where not many writers ever get to. You recognize the complexities. Your stories aren't so much about the events as the feelings of the characters involved. That is what I love so much. And the feelings can be a mish mosh and that's the way it is. Things can be terrible and turn out badly, but what you say, over and over again, is that things don't always happen the way they're supposed to. And there's not much we can do about it. But still, you always have a spark of hope, even in describing horrible events. I'm not sure how to describe it or define it. But you always get to the emotions. And you have this love and tenderness for what you write about. It's like you're a rabbi filled with compassion. And that spark is what I've come here to try and obtain. If nothing else, you can write this all up in one of your stories. I've come to you because I believe in you. I have a therapist and I believe in her too. I mean, I believe in that process. But I thought to make contact with you. I don't know if what I'm asking for is advice or just some consoling. But this is stuff you deal with in your writing all the time. I know there's not just some simple answer. Like winning the lottery."

"I have an idea of what you're talking about," I interrupted. "I don't pretend to know anything out of the ordinary."

"I don't have a story to tell you. I grew up in New Jersey in a house my grandfather built and in which my father grew up. An ordinary childhood. Nothing profound. Off to college. A year traveling around Europe. Home with no idea what to do. I fell in with a group of poets and writers in the East Village and thought I'd found a family. Support. Literature, it seemed, was our mutual passion. But now I think it was the lifestyle I was most attracted to, not the creative act. No responsibility. Nothing was important but writing and, of course, having a good time. So we were all just very reckless for years. A lot of drinking, drugs, as much sex as possible, which was never enough. It was a very promiscuous scene. Decadent. I don't know. Now maybe I'm feeling guilty about time wasted. I didn't write any masterpieces. I had some recognition and gave readings. That gave me a sense of worth I'd never had before. With writing I could attempt to make sense. Though it was all chaos and frazzled energy, in a story or poem I could at least describe some of that. Venting some of that steam soothed me. I also liked to think of myself as an artist. I thought that made me special. But now I look back and think I was kidding myself. I wasn't in touch."

"It sounds to me like you're being hard on yourself, David," I said. "A young person shouldn't be obliged to know what they want. That is a time for looking around. It sounds to me that you were fortunate to have that opportunity."

"Yes, I think so too. But now I am no longer a youngster. I still don't have any idea of what's to be done. I feel as if now I am obliged to accomplish something. Do something with my life. All I can manage is to make my living. Nothing seems exciting to me anymore. I have no commitment to anything. Everything seems transitory. It seems to me that nothing really matters. I know you quote Spinoza on occasion, or other skeptics who question the day-to-day edicts of the Jewish books. I'm not quite ready to give in to my despair though that seems like the easiest thing to do. I still want to live. I know there's no simple solution to this sort of questioning. I'm not about to head into Jewish law. Maybe it's because I'm too proud, but I can't accept obedience of rituals as the answer. I don't know what I expect from this meeting. I know you say what you have to say in your books. But I feel desperate. I'm not about to leap out the window. Don't get alarmed. I know things go on and we get through. But I want to feel alive again.

Not just go through the motions. I don't want to reach old age and feel I've squandered the blessedness of life."

What could I tell this young man? Who gave me the right to say anything? As if anything I had to say might matter. I'd done what I had to do throughout my life. Because I sometimes could get excited and not stop myself from saying what was on my mind, I'd influence people occasionally. Some I left in worse shape. One or two I helped. I didn't want to tell this young person what he needed was, in essence, a kick in the rear and to just open his eyes to what was around him. I'm not a scientist. There's no cure I can prescribe. And I can't pretend to understand what a person 40 years younger than myself is experiencing. Times have changed for us all. When I was 20, leaving my little village in Poland for Warsaw with its writers' union and intellectual exuberance, with ideas being tossed around that made it seem like fresh frosting on a cake, I could see history changing. I was happy to have something to replace the strict regime of my Jewish studies. I was a troublemaker. I don't know what made me the skeptic. Somehow my eyes were open. I rejected obedience and was excited by the idea of free will. What can I say? But I was beginning to understand this young man's dilemma. Back in Warsaw, we had hope. Even through the horrors of Hitler, an aberration no one should experience again, something told us this is an outrage against humanity. We still had a sense that in the scheme of things this was a terrible blemish and that collectively there was some good left to put an end to this.

What this young man was complaining about was a loss of hope. And that is something I couldn't easily restore to him.

"David, you believe your life is askew. That it's not where it's supposed to be. This is a difficult thing to change. But, let me tell you something. Hope is not something you win in a lottery game. It's good you come to see me to let me know, to try to share this with me. I can understand you a little bit. But I must tell you there's not a lot I can tell you. I've written stories my entire life. That is how I have dealt with things. It's not a bad way."

We sat there for a moment in silence. I watched him as he thought things over. He had forgotten that I was in the room with him and stared ahead at nothing. The drama made me uncomfortable. This person was demanding too much of me. What he expected from me was beyond my power. A nudge is all I could give. My mind raced back through my memory to my own youth in Europe. I was sympathetic to this man's questions. He'll have to figure it out himself, I thought. I was in a fix. Here was this person coming to me for advice because he'd read my books and found solace in them. But I'm not a wizard who can grant wishes or even answer difficult questions. So this person who'd come to me, who trusted me for some guidance, what was I to do? There was nothing I could think to say. It looked like this was going to be one of those times things didn't turn out so well. A clue, a glimpse of hope is what this young man was asking me for.

"If there were some easy answer," I told him, "someone would be making a lot of money. I'll look at your story," I said, to bring our meeting to an end. Perhaps that would be enough of a promise to reassure him for the time being. He recognized the signal and got up and managed a smile.

"Mr. Singer, I can't tell you how grateful I am that you agreed to see me. I know there's no easy answer to what I'm telling you about. But I'm glad you show interest. Maybe that's all I can reasonably expect from anyone."

He wasn't a dumb fellow, my visitor. I saw him to the door. We shook hands and I returned to the living room and surveyed the piles of paper with a sigh. I sat down and thought for a moment about this meeting. Had I handled it all right? Did I show enough caring? Would David think I was too dismissive? That was so unlike my stories. How could I live up to my reputation all the time?

Well, I picked up the manuscript of David's stories lying next to me on the sofa. I thought of putting up water for tea but my eyes were attracted to the typewriting. I began reading the first story. It was called "The Visitor" and began, "Occasionally, I get a call from someone who has read my stories..."

What I Should Have Said to Jimmy Fallon

I took this selfie a week or two ago. Let me find it. Hold on. Here it is. Me holding the new issue of *Vanity Fair* with you on the cover. I was going to post it on Facebook to get you some exposure – because you need it. As if you haven't been in the papers every day.

How's it going? You have this week off before starting the new show? Oh man, it's going to be awesome. Listen, I know you've probably been watching tape of Johnny Carson. I know you, you're a good student of comedy. I know you've prepared. But, you're too young to have watched him each day growing up like I did. Man, he was part of my life for years. Every night at 11:30, turn on the TV for Johnny. I can be honest with you, right? It was glitzy and all, and there was something alluring and appealing about being a part of the proceedings – as if by observing I was part of this exclusive club – but, I don't think I liked him very much as a person. I certainly didn't like his clothes. His suits were too conservative for my taste, too off the rack. Which is something I've been meaning to discuss with you. And Doc's suits, yikes. The show was entertaining and all, right? I mean he was so polished delivering the opening monolog you just had to believe him. He was in such command it didn't matter if a joke bombed, he'd get through it just with that attitude. And that's really all that mattered, his momentum up there, taking over our lives for those first 15 minutes.

Your suits, by the way. I'd like to take you shopping and get you some better suits. You're wearing so much gray and black, industrial colors. It's like the cube partitions in my office – those color tones calculated to induce some psychological response to keep us from hopping over the partition and strangling each other.

But anyway, what I wanted to tell you was I had this great job in high school. I think it was the best job I ever had, driving a delivery car for Chicken Delight. Does that chain even exist anymore? It was the best fried chicken. I drove a VW Beetle with the passenger seat removed and a metal box placed in there. There was Sterno at the bottom keeping the food warm – an open flame in a rolling tuna fish can. That was safe. I drove all over making deliveries in the evenings after school and on the weekends. Boy, I knew those roads in Passaic, Clifton, Rutherford, Garfield. I knew the best routes to get from A to B, when to hop on the Parkway and pay the 10 cents. I loved driving that car, even into the rough neighborhoods. People were so happy getting their chicken. I guess I made tips and all. I don't think I even cared. What did I know about money management. The point, I suppose, was that I was working my ass off, gaining a work ethic. It made me responsible. Or kept me out of trouble, more likely. Otherwise I definitely would've been with my friends smoking pot or be toking up in my bedroom listening to Chicago or Sly and the Family Stone or WNEW-FM.

OK, here's what I want to tell you. Those months were the greatest. I finished around 11, settled up with the owners, Otto and what was her name? She had a nice German accent, like Zsa Zsa Gabor. Hungarian, I know. Then I get in my dad's Rambler American, four on the floor, the best car ever, and drive back into downtown to visit my girlfriend. It was like a one-minute drive, maybe two. I park and go upstairs to her apartment. Her parents were always in the bedroom asleep. I never saw them. My girlfriend – her name was Lucy – was gorgeous and the sweetest. She was so nice and it just knocks me out that she so obviously seemed to like me. I didn't quite get it, but it felt good. Well, we put on Johnny Carson, watch maybe a minute and then have sex on the living room couch. With her folks down the hall in their bedroom with the door closed, either oblivious or giving us privacy to allow me to shtup their daughter during Johnny Carson. He always had to be on, it was part of the ritual. It wasn't the greatest sex for her. I mean, it was fantastic for me, but she pretty much just let me do what I had to do. I didn't know anything about pleasing her or connecting as a couple. This was just raw, selfish teenage sex. I was happy.

What I know now, what is it, 45 years later. How I'd like to see her again. But, I can't. Here's the deal. She's in the witness protection program. She came to say goodbye to me after I graduated college and moved into New York. At that point, she had a Pontiac Firebird with an eagle painted all in flaming colors on the hood, what a car. She drove into the city to meet me. I didn't know what was happening. I thought it was just a visit. We made out a little bit, but then she told me she would be entering the witness protection program. This is all happening too fast. I thought we might be rekindling our romance, but then she was gone.

The boyfriend she had after me was involved in a murder. I was a suspect for a minute, she told me, but I was in Europe at the time. I went for a year after I graduated college. I'll tell you about that another time. It was the best. Lonely at times, but boy were my eyes open and ready for anything. And sex when you're traveling, that's a whole other story. You're so relaxed. You're automatically in the same situation as everyone you meet and you're meeting people your own age mostly to run around to museums and walk around and have meals together, wine in the evenings.

So, yeah, your suits. I'd like to see you in softer fabrics, Italian linens. I'm sure your suits now are fitted, but with some softer fabrics I think you'd look classier, more stylish. And you could wear some color, a pale blue tie. Try green. It'd be fun to go with you to one of those places to get a suit made, like that scene in *Dumb and Dumber* when the guys are getting tuxes custom-made. But, I'm thinking more Miles Davis than Lloyd and what's his face. Can we do that?

My Folks Dispel of Their Earthly Presence

I couldn't have been in a more idyllic spot when the bad news arrived. The view from my friends' place in the Catskills stretched down a valley, across Route 28, to a mountain range rising in the distance. Decades ago I hiked trails over those ridges – Slide, Cornell, Wittenberg – so my familiarity with the area was always a comfort. But this call from my mother was something else. I was surprised that we even had cell phone reception where we were, but the call came in around 4 p.m. Perfect timing too, it'd turn out. Considerate.

"Your father didn't wake up," she said. Her mind was zapped from radiation treatments and her speech, I was beginning to accept, was starting to get a bit strange.

"He's dead?," I asked.

The whole scenario unfolding was enough to make me sit. Remarkably, for the seriousness of the moment, my seat was the front porch of an A-frame cabin, and the view, a vista comprised of thousands of trees, sort of helped me process the details, which were making only half sense. Why had it taken my mom almost the entire day to phone me with the news. Normally, she would have called as soon as she was done calling the EMS or whatever has to be done. Instead, in the condition she now was in, the usual expectations were disappearing. It'd take me a few more months to figure it out, but she too was fading from existence, the consequence of cancer diagnosed a month earlier.

The trip back to the city was quiet. My friends were as kind and gentle as one would hope, but what is there to say. I felt bad about spoiling the weekend with my family crisis but at least the timing was right. We had begun to get ready to drive back at the time anyway. So, there was that.

Following the trip down to Florida for my father's memorial service, the next four months were polluted for me with the disintegration of my mother. Several trips back and forth, arranging care, phone calls with lawyers, bankers, their friends. She was not in pain, that was reassuring. Plus, I was deluded for a while, still, that she might get better. Totally unreasonable, but her doctors didn't tell me otherwise.

I insisted on hiring a caregiver even though she said she didn't need one. When the agency first sent Marie over for an interview, we sat around the kitchen table in the blatant light and chatted. Within a few moments, Marie started talking about her admiration for Louis Farrakhan. This is terrific, I thought. If my mother had been in her right mind that would have been the extent of the conversation. But, meaning was eluding my mother by this point. She sat there quietly and I nodded my head and hired Marie, impressed that she could talk so freely about her values, even when they might conflict with those of her potential employer. But more, I was just relieved and grateful to have someone willing to move in to attend to my mom's needs, another task checked off the list.

Each morning while I was there, my mother emerged from her bedroom with a smile, what was left of her body weight supported by the walker she needed now. It was as if even in her deterioration, she was still taking care of me, pretending still that everything was going to be all right. It wasn't a phony reassurance. Her morning cheer was sincere. I knew that. She was truly delighted to see me, and I was glad to see her doing so well, a chance for recovery still an ingredient of the passing days.

My opportunity to have some quality time with her was disappearing, however. Now that my father was gone, I thought, at least now I might be able to establish a connection that had evaded me for half a century.

He was impossible, I'd decided awhile back. Perhaps it all started to go downhill when I was around four and kicked him in the nuts while goose stepping and giving the Heil Hitler salute. We had this game we played maybe three or four times where we would kick a bar of soap around the bottom of the tub while taking a shower together. It was the most fun interaction we ever had. Then, he'd lift me up and place me on top of the closed toilet to towel me off. I don't know where I learned this, but at that intimate moment I raised my arm straight out in a fervent salute while kicking up my leg in fine military style. I can't imagine what shocked him more: That his freshly showered infant son, who'd been circumcised in all the ritualistic trappings of the Hebrew tradition only three years previously, would be suddenly swearing allegiance to the Nazi party, or that this committed Nazi just delivered a kick to his exposed organ. I remember the surprised look on his face.

Unfortunately, there was no discussion. He didn't ask why I had decided to switch sides. No great father-son talk resulted. He just finished toweling me off in silence and we were out of there. A man who had spent four years in the U.S. Navy and undergone untold horrors in theaters of action in Europe and the South Pacific, faced with the realization that all he fought for had come to naught in the bathroom of his own home. Despite the struggles resulting in the blessings of his achievements, his second-born son, in whom he likely held the highest hopes and aspirations, the progeny on whom could be measured his success as a middle-class American, had betrayed not only his domestic obligation, but his religion and country as well. It was perhaps at that moment, before even intellectual disagreements factored in, that he lost his hope of connecting to me in any relevant way.

But my mother, I thought, somewhere in that character was the empathetic being waiting to emerge – given the freedom it needed. What a partnership she and him had been. For me, though, it was always like a tag team match attempting to communicate with them on any but a superficial level, except I had no partner. I was always still the kid in the backseat without a voice, without representation.

Perhaps now my mother and I might have earned the right to a comfort that had always been out of reach. The big guy was gone. "The Générale," my mother and I called him on occasion, one of our more daring and rare alliances. But, instead of a shared closeness, I was finding myself in the position of having to take charge. Me, who'd always avoided responsibility as much as possible. Who strove for obscurity. Who once thought of forming a Losers' Club, but didn't want a leadership position. How peculiar to have roles reversed. With synapses in her brain short-circuited from treatments, my mother's mind was curtailed. It was fascinating to observe – she was like a sweet zombie – but disappointing to have our chance for closeness kicked down the road forever.

Ever try teaching a woman who just lost her husband of 60+ years how to use the remote to switch from TV to DVD? Her brain cells were fading like the HAL computer in *2001* having its memory panels stolen away. I expended the effort though it didn't take long to see this was absurd. Things were beyond my control. Reason and rational behavior, to which I tethered my movement through life with desperate conviction, was no longer applicable. For me, showing up at the correct airport gate at the right time was the ultimate achievement, the truest proof of a reasonable universe where geolocation and time intersected in a just and beautiful collaboration. For this situation, there were no maps, no GPS.

In fact, her mind was so affected that after my father's memorial she'd never mention him again. I tried to get her to talk, to have an adult discussion, but she wasn't capable. I'd just sit on the couch with her and hold her hand. She could make it known that she liked ice cream and not much else. But there was still a sparkle in her eyes. And she was still mobile, if with some assistance. It was obvious she liked receiving visitors. Her friends in the "active adult" condo development, Sun Valley East, came in to sit with her. She'd earned respect from some of the neighbors having done years of committee work and played hundreds of rounds of Mahjong and Pinochle in the club house. And participated in water aerobics every morning and played tennis two or three times a week until just recently. Buy better sneakers, I'd advised ineffectively.

It's good to have a cancer doctor in the family at a time like this. My cousin, internationally renowned gastrointestinal oncologist Dr. Richard M. Goldberg, happened to be in Miami for a conference and made the two-hour drive north to check in on my mom, apparently consulting with her doctors. He knew the prognosis was bad and mentioned it to his dad, my Uncle Bernie, who in a telephone conversation with me conveyed the stark fact: My mother was dying. I wasn't prepared for this news.

"Why are you telling me this," I responded, breaking down.

"You have to know," he said in as kind and gentle a tone as is possible.

Maybe it was a week that went by. I was out of tears and still too dazzled by all that was transpiring when I received the call alerting me of her death. It was 2 a.m. with the simple announcement from Marie, who'd been with her 24/7 for four months: "She's passed." An extra syllable in the lilt of her Caribbean accent. An hour later a sheriff called to check off some formality, and I made arrangements to head back down there.

This time, for my return engagement at the Beth Israel Memorial Chapel, I asked the rabbi to read my eulogy to the crowd filling up the chapel. I'd blubbered my way through the remarks for my dad's memorial four months earlier.

And then a few days spent dispensing stuff from the apartment with trips to the UPS Store to ship treasures to family all over the country. I offered my parents' friends whatever they wanted. One took my mom's beloved Lladró figurines. It was a pleasure to donate my dad's art books to the library. I thought the clubhouse would be pleased to receive some of my dad's paintings, but it was like a political committee in there with a bunch of gruff seniors ingrained in their own agendas. So, a few went to friends and a final bunch went to one of the maintenance guys. He seemed delighted to receive them and I was pleased to distribute them to someone who appreciated my dad's art and my largesse.

Clothes and dishes went to the Goodwill and everything else went to Marie. Her son came over and we loaded the stereo, TV, computer and other stuff into his Chevy. Plus, I gave them my folks' Mercury. In a miracle of the universe's kindness, transferring the title took only minutes at the local DMV office.

Soon, there was not much left in their unit. Twenty years ago when they bought the place, the area was all horse farms and orange groves. Now it was an engorged matrix of chain stores and condo developments. Still, my parents were happy in their retirement and it was almost a pleasure for me to visit them – especially once I'd figured out how to complement a few days with them with a trip to Port St. Lucie to watch a Mets spring training game, or a night or two in Miami or, best yet, a solo drive down the Keys blasting U2.

I managed to purge my folks' place of everything but a triangulated American flag bestowed to me by a veterans committee after my dad's ceremony, and two urns. What to do with them? I wasn't about to bring the canisters back to my New York apartment. I had no room, literally, for sentimentality.

The next few days were taken up with lawyers, banks, utilities, condo board, real estate brokers, portfolio managers. I met with them and settled things. My mind wasn't quite lucid. I was going through the motions, showing up on time, signing things. All went smoothly because my folks had made the arrangements. All was tidy and prepared. Also easing the process, it became clear to me that all the professionals with whom I had dealings had been fond of my folks and perhaps granted an extra degree of sympathy and consideration to someone who had just lost both parents within a four-month span.

I settled on the idea of burying their ashes in the small patch of garden in the entryway to their condo unit, but the thought smoldered in my frazzled mind similar to the narrator in "The Tell-Tale Heart." After a few minutes sitting on the couch, I reversed course and dug up the ashes, paranoid that the next owners would plant new flowers, discover the grisly remains and summon the police. I was certainly in Poe territory at this point. Abandoning any sentiment, I resorted to the rational and hauled the ashes across the parking lot, over to the Dumpsters and tossed them in. This didn't sit right either. After a few further moments, I decided the Atlantic Ocean would be appropriate; in fact, brilliant. Driving along A1A, however, it soon became clear that there was no way to launch their ashes into the cosmos anywhere amid those occupied spaces.

I found a semi-secluded spot on the Intracoastal Waterway with a small pier. So, I deposited in there the commingled ashes of Harold Masters, formerly of Passaic, N.J., whose only words about his wartime experience recalled that the sea was red with blood as bodies floated by his Liberty ship off the beach on D-Day, and Mildred Masters née Magidov, a Brooklyn gal, who verified with a checkmark each transaction on the monthly brokerage statement. The location provided an ocean view. Without ceremony, without any honor, just the formality, and back into the car and north to West Palm Beach and the airport. I'd find out in a week or two that I'd lost 20 pounds.

A Note About the Author

When he arrived in Manhattan's East Village in the mid-1970s, Greg Masters pounded rock and roll drums in basement dives, "alternative" spaces, CBGB and Irving Plaza and attended readings and workshops at the Poetry Project at St. Mark's Church and the Nuyorican Poets Cafe. Along with Michael Scholnick and Gary Lenhart, he edited the poetry magazine *Mag City* from 1977-1985. In 1977-78, along with a crew of poet comrades, he produced a cable TV show, *Public Access Poetry*. From 1980-83, he edited the *Poetry Project Newsletter*. He has worked for a number of book, magazine and web publishers, beginning as a proofreader and copy editor and then for the last 20 years as a managing editor. This is his seventh book from Crony Books.

Kind Words for Previous Books

At Maureen's

Greg Masters's writing is so descriptive and candid and perfect.
 – Chris Kraus, author of *Summer of Hate* and *I Love Dick*

For the Artists

Greg Masters brings a streetwise beat reporter's savvy to his assignments. His interviewer's questions are always to the point, intelligently formulated, and tactfully posed.
 – Vincent Katz, poet, author and critic

Three Journals

A masterpiece, a great work featuring powerful journal entries...This is a book that captures the soul and the spirit of the periods it covers with vivid clarity and one cannot help falling in love with the setting, the historical references, the cultural and social commentaries, and the very life throbbing within the narration.
 – Arya Fomonyuy, Readers' Favorite

Three Journals is a literary masterpiece in the nonfiction genre. The vivid portrayal of the author's travels would leave any reader with the desire to get on a plane right away and head to the destinations mentioned in the book. I loved reading the stories and look forward to seeing more from this author. Highly recommended to anyone!

— Danielle Correa, Amazon

A great find. Clear, honest, funny. I was charmed by the author's recollections of his friends and adventures. This is what a journal should be.

— Maria, Amazon

A non-fiction gem! The author and his tales widen the mind and touch the soul. Morocco, The East Village, Mexico... true reality for what makes travel so rewarding. Brilliant author, kind hearted and modest. I loved reading it!

— Amazon customer

A delightful read.

— Alka, Amazon

What All the Songs Add Up To

A must-have book of poems.

— Gog, Amazon

A beautiful book of poems. Greg Masters captures warmth and humor with these carefully crafted little gems.

— Ann F., Amazon